Murder Most C

A Kiss Before Stra

Boo'

By: Γ

Published by:

American Creative Services Publications

Dothan, Alabama

Via Ingram Sparks

Copyright © 2021 by Douglas Sandler.

https://douglassandlerindependentauthor.com/

ISBN: 979869330055

Book cover designed by Fantasyart-6385 through Selfpubbookcover,com

# Introduction

Thank you for buying the fifth book in the A Kiss Before Strangling series. This book covers Police Officer Peter Younger after he returns from United States Army service in WW2 1944-45 Europe then in occupied West Germany 1945-47 returning to the United States in May 1947. He is rehired by the Tillman, Nebraska Police Department.

He picks up where he left off with his girl Sally Painter and the cold streets of Tillman. Little does he know Moloch, Satan, murder, and the occult are back.

Douglas Sandler
Dothan, Alabama
August 2022

IN MEMORY OF MY FAMILY,
Barry Sandler, Uncle
(1938-2020)

David Sandler, Brother
(1963-2020)

Lila Sandler, Mom
(1932-2020)

# Dedication

I dedicate this book to all the readers of all my other books. I also dedicate this book to my goddesses Hecate, Bast, Diana, ISIS, Santa Muerte, and to Lucifer. I also dedicate this book to Gulf Coast State College, Florida State University for helping me be a better writer.

I also dedicate this my eleventh book and the fifth book in the A Kiss Before Strangling series to my professors at Purdue Global On-line University for further helping me write better.

# CHAPTER ONE

Recently discharged Army Lieutenant Peter Younger stood in the locker room of the Tillman Police Department putting on his uniform. Having fought in Europe then doing occupation duty in West Berlin, Germany with the military police. He was glad to be back home as his fellow police officers were happy to see him as was his girl, Sally. The new Police Chief wanted to see him.

He left the locker room and took the elevator to the third floor and was standing in front of the chief's door and knocked and a voice said, "who is it?"

"It's Officer Peter Younger, chief."

"Come on in Officer Younger. Have a seat"

With that Younger opened the door and entered the office. Chief Daniels was a man in his late 50s about 5' 8" with a weight that matched his size, he clearly played football.

Officer Younger closed the door and sat down in a chair nearest his desk and says, "What's up chief?"

I wanted to welcome you back home and let you know all your pay has been deposited into your checking account. I understand your back in the uniform division."

"Yes, I am chief. I like patrolling better than investigating. I also have to get accustomed back to civilian life and in uniform."

"Well, if you need anything let me know."

With that dismissal, Officer Younger left the chief's office to head down to roll call and ran into Detective Mike Knight. "Hi, Mike. Good morning."

"Good morning, Peter. It's great to have you back alive."

As they walk in silence Officer Younger notices Detective Knight is in uniform and when Detective Knight sees the question in Younger's eyes he simply says, "it's a long story, Peter."

After roll call ends the two officers who were partnered drive out of the station parking lot in their late model 1946 Ford patrol car turning up Howland Avenue heading towards Oak Drive to get coffee and breakfast at JP's Coffee House on Seventeenth Street. While they drove Detective Knight says, "I got drunk, and someone started a fight with me and we fought; he then pulled a knife and I shot him. It was ruled justifiable, but I got sent to uniform. I'm in uniform for the next two years and if I drink again, I am fired."

"Sorry to hear that, Mike. If you need to talk or any help, just ask."

"Thanks, Peter I appreciate that."

"Were partners and partners got each other's backs."

While drinking coffee and eating a bagel at the coffee house after twenty-five minutes on May 7, 1947, the dispatcher calls. "Car 7. Car 7 come in."

Office now Corporal Younger picks up the walkie-talkie and replies, "Go ahead dispatch, car 7 here."

"Go to 753 Sixth Street call of domestic violence, response code 3."

"Rodger dispatch. Car 7 going code 3 to 753 Sixth Street."

With that, the two cops run to the car and as they get in Detective Knight hits the overheads and speeds off. It takes them ten minutes to arrive and as they hear yelling coming from the house as they get to the front door Detective Knight yells, "POLICE OPEN THE DOOR NOW." There is no response and with more yelling, he busts the door down.

As they enter the living room, they see a bloody woman standing over a man unconscious on the floor bleeding from the ears and head. As the woman drops the bat and falls into a chair Corporal Younger call the ambulance.

Corporal Younger runs over to the woman and Detective Knight goes to the man. After ten minutes three other cops arrive with the ambulance crew. They load the man and woman into the ambulance with a uniform it heads to the hospital. After forty minutes they leave and go 10-8 which is back in service.

It was the morning of 7 May 1947 in another part of Tillman a woman named Julie Danvers age 35 second daughter of a wealthy banker. Her dad owned the town bank. She wanted to earn her own money and not live off her parents. She was a seamstress who did work for the other wealthy families. The Park Slope scandal: she took valuables from those families. She was suspected, but it was never proven. She got pregnant out of wedlock, and it scandalized her family and the town.

She left Tillman for Baxter and met and married a well-to-do tradesman in May 1948. Two months later he committed suicide and left a note. Friends and family found it strange and suspected her of his death. At the will reading on 7 August 1948 the husband's family contested her being in the will and the probate judge after a thirty-minute pause sided with the family and gave the estate to them only giving her $9000 plus one-year funds to care for the child. Four weeks later the child died mysteriously. She met Samuel Patterson and from September 1948 to October 1948 they did a blackmail scam where she found wealthy married men and slept with them then her co-criminal would burst in playing her husband; accuse the man and threatened to show his wife the pictures if they were not paid. The pair earned $50,000 in five weeks and on 17 October 1948, her co-conspirator was found shot in the head in his 1940 ford coupe with a suicide. On 13 November after the verdict, she fled Nebraska.

The morning of November 14th after the police got a warrant for her arrest. Corporal Peter Younger was eating breakfast at the Burger Barn with fellow Police Officer Jim Leeds. They talked about their time in the army, and they traded stories about their girlfriends. At 09 30 hours, the handheld radio went off.

The dispatcher said, "Car 8, car 8 10-43 26872 64th Street handle code two." Corporal Younger picked up the handheld as he and Leeds ran out saying "car 8 rodger. ETA 15 minutes." They reached the patrol car got in and hit the overheads and sped to the assault in progress. As they sped to the assault in progress, they wondered who would be out in a 7-degree cold windy morning. As they pulled up, they saw a figure in a thick coat hitting a woman. They stopped and jumped out and Officer Leeds yelled "GET OFF HER and against the wall."

The figure stopped and suddenly turned to the cops and raised his hand which held a large stick and before the man could do anything Corporal Younger had him on the ground cuffing him as Officer Leeds tended to the woman. Suddenly, the woman shoved Officer Leeds away and pulled out a large knife charging him yelling "Lauxnome de nia dio satand la diejj brilanta, mi glutos vlan animon" He yelled twice for her to stop, and three shots rang out and she fell dead.

As Corporal Younger picked the man up and looked at his partner he asked, "What the hell happened?"

"I, I, don't know Peter?" Officer Leeds replied.

Corporal Younger turns to the man and says "Just who the hell are you? Do you know what's going on?"

"My name is Father Joseph Umberto of the Office of Exorcist's Archdiocese of Chicago. I was trying to talk to her and bring her home to her family when she started to fight me."

"Who is she?" Officer Leeds asked.

"Her name is Lisa Dianetello of Chicago Illinois, and she vanished five months ago after joining a small group of satanic worshipers who soon fled Chicago to avoid prosecution for several assaults. There is a loose group of Satanists, and I tracked them here and by chance spotted her."

"What were you going to do if you got her back to Chicago?" Officer Leeds asked.

"Deprogram her. The group she belongs to the satanic family which is a group of followers of William Lorax who believes if he finds the chosen woman to give to their god he will live forever. Other satanic groups disavow him as too evil even for them." Father Umberto replied.

After the crime techs took their pictures and the coroner removed the body, the blood-soaked snow was washed down the sewer by a fire-hose. The two officers took the priest to the station to finish the interview and make sure he was who he said he was.

They released the father nine hours later after confirming who he was and the facts. Officers Leeds and Younger asked Chief Jim Carter and they were joined by Assistant Chief Allen Liebermann in the squad room and went over what they knew so far, at 2:30 p.m. they broke the meeting up and the two officers went back on patrol.

Corporal Younger got a mysterious phone call on Friday night at p p.m... He answered the phone "Corporal Younger, Tillman Police can I help you?"

A voice asked "Can I speak to you alone? Say 10:302 pm at the corner of Seventy-fourth Street and Third Avenue. I have some information to give you and I don't want the others to know, or I am dead."

"OK! Can I get your name?"

"Julie." The line went dead. He sat in the squad room and five minutes later. He picked up the phone and dialed the detective's squad. After three rings the phone answered "Robbery/homicide, Detective Dan Hamilton."

"Yes, Detective Hamilton. This is Corporal Younger in patrol I received a disturbing phone call and I'd like to talk to you about it."

"Yes, I can be down in four minutes." The detective said and the phone went dead. Detective Hamilton walked into the squad room and went up too Corporal Younger and said, "how can I help you corporal?"

"Well, Detective Hamilton I and my partner have an assault and battery involving a priest and a woman and my partner had to kill the woman who attacked him. When we questioned the priest, he said he was trying to return the woman home and out of an evil satanic cult.

Now I get this mysterious phone call asking me to meet her because she wants to give me information on this cult but is scared the others would kill her."

"Did she say come alone?"

"No, she did not."

"Well, I'll come with you to give you backup and she can talk to both of us; what time did she say?"

"10:30p.m. tonight corner of Seventy-Fourth and Third." It was 10 p.m. when they left the police station to get there early to scout the location.

They got there fifteen minutes early, parked one block south watching the corner with binoculars. They saw a girl in a long jacket hiding in the dark doorway. They decided to drive up turning on the police dome light and pulled up turning it off. The girl approached. He rolled down the window saying, "I'm Corporal Younger and this is Detective Hamilton how can we help you?"

As she got in the back of the unmarked ford she said, "can you drive as we talk I don't want anyone to know I am talking to you." They drove off.

Detective Hamilton turns to the woman and asks the woman "What information do you have?"

"I am a member of the Temple of Moloch and our founder Dr. Edward Malcom who now goes by the name of William Lorax leads about ten followers who do sacrifices to Moloch. At first, he did illegal abortions using the fetuses and after he was forced to flee Chicago in 1929, he settled in New York City in 1930 and kidnapped street children till again he was forced to flee in 1933. He traveled always on the run till he arrived in Omaha in 1947. If you check, there you will find child disappearances and he came here to Tillman in June 1947. He got three of his rabid supporters pregnant delivered their children and sacrificed them."

"Do you know where he and his followers are now?" Corporal Younger asked.

"He's laying low, so he doesn't get caught. I know two addresses, but he may have others I know nothing about."

"Why do you do this anonymously?" Detective Hamilton asked.

"I heard that a member of the county sheriff's office is a member, and I don't know his name, but this needs to be done because I can't do this anymore."

"Where do you want us to drop you off?" Corporal Younger asked.

"Can you arrest and book me for vagrancy so me being with you won't raise red flags."

They take her to the station and book her for vagrancy. She's taken before the night court judge, and she pleads guilty saying she needed a warm place to sleep. An older man steps forward "Judge I am William Lorax a friend of hers and I'll give her a place to stay and this won't happen again."

"Very well. I fine you fifteen dollars and suspend your sentence. Don't let me see you again young lady."

"Yes, your honor." With that, the two leave and go up to the chief's office to fill him in considering now a deputy sheriff is involved. Five minutes later Corporal Younger, Detective Hamilton, Chief Carter, Mayor Berg are in the chief's office.

Mayor Berg turns to Corporal Younger "What does this have to do with the woman your partner had to kill?"

"Well, Mayor Berg the woman's involvement goes deeper. I just told you the meeting me and Detective Hamilton had it seems we have a group of disavowed satanic cultists who have a history of child sacrifices led by a psycho somewhere in Tillman who have a deputy sheriff as a member."

The chief asked, "Do we know who this deputy is?"

Corporal Younger replied, "no we do not." The mayor asks, "Do we tell the sheriff about this?"

"No, we do not." The chief says.

In an old house across town, a room is glowing by candlelight and the woman sacrifice was tied to the altar and four men and one woman took off their robes and the woman and one man pulled on a pair of rubber gloves and rubber butchers' aprons as they would do the sacrifice. Even though the woman was gaged she tried to scream. One of the men rang a bell as the high priestess said "Lauxnome de niadio satano la peij brilanta; in the name of our god Moloch please accept this sacrifice".

The woman named Stoney picked up a sharp knife as did the man and after they cut through all the skin and fat and muscle and exposed the bone, they each picked up bone saws and as the buzz grew louder the blade cut through the bone in three minutes and they removed her arms. The floor and the ceiling was covered in blood and gore as were their aprons and gloves. The girl then took her bloody knife and cut through her chest and peeled back the skin and muscle back to expose her rib cage and using the bone saw cut through her ribs and pulled out her beating heart and held it in the air saying, "Moloch accept this heart as our offering." She then dropped it into a flaming cauldron, and it sizzled. So ended the life of the girl named Julie.

After the girl was dismembered in ten black plastic garbage bags along with the gloves, aprons they had them dumped in a dumpster four blocks east. They used bleach to clean the bone saw, altar, floor, and ceiling. They then had an orgy.

Father Joseph Umbertlo of the Order of Exorcists was meeting daily with the Tillman Police to help stop the evil cult. On Monday, October 18, 1948 Corporal Peter Younger received a call of a dead body located on the eastside of Parkland Park. Corporal Younger and his partner Officer Leeds responded and upon arriving saw Detective Hamilton and as they approached he said, "Its Father Umbertlo Peter, he's been murdered, and his body dumped." The coroner arrived and didn't even have to examine the body he ruled it a homicide; it was clear at the scene the bullet hole in the head and a missing heart was clear.

At the official autopsy there was found a blood type other than the father's A-. It was O+ and there were blond hairs on his clothes. Seven hours later Corporal Peter Younger was standing over another dead body, this one in several black trash bags and wondered who murdered the young girl. The coroner looked at the torso and pointed out over one hundred stab and slashes. Corporal Younger recognized the face. Her name was Julie Watson, the seventeen-year-old daughter of local banker and city council member Tommy "Billy Joe" Watson. Corporal Younger knew the family and knew the girl was not one to get into trouble even though she ran away several times and was found last year in Chicago and returned home.

The police interviewed several people who a patrol officer detained till the detectives arrived. As the interviews went on a description of the possible killer emerged and Corporal Younger told Detective Hamilton, "I believe I know who they are describing. Her name is Susan Alexander a/k/a Stoney who is the high priestess of the temple of Moloch."

"Do you have any idea where she is now?" Detective Hamilton asked.

"I have two possible addresses we can stake out to see if she shows up."

"Let's do it asap Corporal Younger."

# Chapter Two

As Corporal Younger and Detective Hamilton drove to the first address, a seedy house located at 360 Seventy-fifth Street and since they were in an undercover car, they put out a code 5 which means stakeout marked units stay away. It was 5 pm when they arrived stopping one block from the house. Two other detectives were staking out the second address 6430 Central Blvd.

It was 9 p.m. when Corporal Younger spotted a man leaving the house carrying three garbage bags and put them in a car's trunk. Younger and Hamilton followed the man and had a uniform do a traffic stop. As the police officer hit his lights the car tried to speed off but hit a patch of black ice and skidded and hit a light pole and since cars didn't have seat belts and safety glass he crashed through the windshield and landed in a bloody heap.

As other police cars pulled up to 360 Seventy-fifth Street and ran into the house Detective Hamilton ran over to the injured man and as he tried to save his life he asked, "Why did you run?"

"There is a body mutilated in the bags and I wanted to escape and dispose of them, but I'm now dead." With that the man died.

The coroner had the body removed and since the cause of death was obvious case closed. The body in the garbage bags was another issue. One of the cops called for the detectives to enter the house. They did and they recoiled when they saw the temple. It was the walls painted red the blood-stained altar in the candlelight it was straight out of a horror movie. The police photographer took pictures, and they searched the house. Except for a room with mattresses used for sleeping and the temple room it was empty.

Corporal Youngers stood in the temple and felt a cold shuddering chill rising up his back and he felt an oppressive feeling and was worried that something that was summoned could attack and follow him. He picks up his walkie talkie and pushed the button saying, "This is Corporal Younger dispatch; could you have Father Allen McCarter dispatched to this address asap?"

The dispatcher replied, "Rodger. Will call him." As they waited for the father to arrive. Lieutenant Miller said, "Peter? We need to stop this sick bastard before someone else dies."

Younger asks, "Lieutenant, can we wait on the front porch? As I hate the feeling in here."

They stood on the front porch Father McCarter arrived with his assistant and they went into the house. As they entered a dark presence showed up and tried to attack the two priests. Father McCarter held up a cross in one hand and a vile of holy water and flung it at the demon yelling, "I command you in the name of Jesus, father, son and holy ghost to leave and return to where you came from."

The cracking of energy in the temple was thick and the air boiled as the fight went on. Younger thought he saw two figures, one black and evil fighting with one pure white. The demon screamed in some unknown language and the priests in Latin and after twenty minutes it fled and the stench of sulfur and evil cold feeling was gone. The evidence techs gathered up the stuff they needed, and everyone left.

Corporal Younger asked a cop named Thomas who was on the vice squad and asked him, "Do you know any occult people in town?"

"Well Peter there is a woman named Leslie Pattched who is a white witch and owns an occult shop in town. She stays low key, so as not to draw attention to her practices. Her shop is located at 6410 Sixty-fourth Street; tell her Thomas sent you and she'll help."

Corporal Younger got in his unmarked patrol car and headed to the witch's shop. He pulled up to a non-descript brownstone two story shop and parked out front and went in. He pressed the buzzer and chimes sounded somewhere inside. Nothing happened for four minutes and then the door opened a crack and a voice from within said, "Who is it?"

Younger flashed his badge the universal passkey and said, "Corporal Younger, Tillman PD. I have some questions for Leslie Pattched. Officer Thomas sent me."

The door opened wider, to reveal a statuesque young woman dressed in a flowing white caftan with thick dark hair framed her lovely face. She had an open neckline of the caftan hinted at what Younger suspected would be ample cleavage. Younger was pleasantly surprised, since he had come half expecting to find an aging crone with wiry hair and wart on her nose.

He glanced quickly at her naked ring finger before deciding how to address her. "Miss Pattched?"

"Yes." She answered, flashing a disarming smile. "Can I help you?"

"I hope so." He answered frankly. "I have a few questions I'd like to ask you. Again, Officer Thomas sent me."

Her eyebrow formed a graceful arch. "Really?" How interesting won't you come in?"

Younger brushed past her into a large room furnished with tasteful elegance. He had no set conception of what a witch's home should look like, but he saw nothing immediately out of place within that living room. His eyes scanned the open doorways that ringed that room, finally catching a glimpse of what appeared to be an altar, against the far wall of an adjoining bedroom. The woman followed his gaze and noticed the object of his interest. "Is something wrong Mr....er...Younger, was it?"

Younger answered, "No. Nothing wrong. I'm interested in your altar."

She looked surmised, "Oh? Are you a practitioner?"

"No, I'm afraid my interest is purely professional."

The woman sobered slightly. "I see, I don't see. Has the state revived its law against witchcraft?"

Younger shook his head. "I was thinking of the laws against murder."

She looked startled and confused. "I'm afraid I still don't understand." She said.

Younger explained, "I'm investigating a killing that took place at 380 Seventy-fifth Street."

The young woman pondered that for a long moment, her face finally showing dawning recognition. "Seventy-fifth Street? Yes, I believe I read something about that in the paper; there weren't many details I'm afraid."

"That was no accident. We recovered evidence at the scene which suggested that the killers had some occult motive for the crime."

"Oh?" She smiled impishly at him. "am I a suspect, Corporal Younger?"

Younger answered her smile with one of his own. "No, you're not at the moment I'm here because word on the street has you down as the lady to see for answers about witchcraft and related topics."

"That depends on the questions, I should think." She responded.

"Okay, fair enough. I'm looking for people who like their mumbo-jumbo with a side of blood."

The young woman's expression was serious almost grim. "It isn't wise to mock things you don't understand; many people regard that mumbo-jumbo as a religion, even a lifestyle."

Younger spread his hands in a placating gesture. "I'm not out to stifle anyone's freedom of expression, unless that self-expression happens to include felony homicide Miss Pattched."

"Call me Leslie."

Younger forged ahead, ignoring the interruption. "Are you aware of any group whose ritual might include a sacrifice?"

Again she wore a startled face. "Human sacrifice? Why no...I mean...it's Rather difficult to say, without..." Younger waited patiently while she collected her thoughts and then continued, "Can you tell me anything about the evidence you found?"

Younger shrugged, "A dismembered body with a sexual twist. There were some black candles and an inverted pentagram."

Miss Pattched shook her head, "They're standard equipment for black witches."

It was Younger's turn to raise a curious eyebrow, "You segregate your witches?"

The woman laughed softly, "Not the way you mean. There are white and black practitioners. The designation depends upon one's choice of a deity and attitude toward evil."

"I see." Younger said. His tone making it plain that he didn't understand at all.

Her corporation vanished and she asked him to leave. As he left she said low sexy tone, "If you want to fuck me just ask. I also practice sex magic." As he left, his face red, he heard her laughing. Since it was late Younger went home as he had to go to the trial of Susan Alexander.

# Chapter Three

The inquest began at 9 a.m. on 21 November 1948 in the county courthouse with Judge Kingsley running it. Paul Miller, the defense attorney for Susan Alexander and Bob Baker the city attorney and the fifteen-person inquest jury was seated.

The judge gave the city attorney permission to go first. "We expect to show that the defendant Susan Alexander was responsible for the death and dismembering of the decedent and that her behavior at her arrest was fiction designed to get sympathy. We will argue that you find she was responsible for his death and there is enough to convict of first-degree murder."

Judge Kingsley asked the defendant if she wanted to make a statement and her lawyer Mr. Miller replied, "No, your honor. We will reserve our statement later. Since it is the city attorneys' job to prove the guilt of the defendant beyond reasonable doubt, and if the evidence fails we will rely upon that failure to prove her innocence."

Judge Kingsley replied "That will do gentleman. I don't want remarks to the court. Mr. prosecutor. The defendant has waved an opening statement at this time, Put on your first witness."

"My first witness is Tom Butler." Tom Butler took the oath and disclosed that he was a deputy coroner. That he had been called to the eastside of Parkland Park when the body of Father Joseph Umbertlo had been discovered at about 9:15 p.m. on the night of October Eighteenth, 1948."

He had taken charge of the proceedings he identified various photographs showing the position of the body and the location where it had been found. "I examined the body and then after photos were taken the body was taken to the coroner's office where the cloths had been removed and an autopsy had been done. Again photos had been taken of the body during the several stages of the autopsy and they are on the second chart." Bob Baker announced that the photographs are very gruesome as he showed them to the jury, several members of the inquest jury had a green look on their faces but stayed.

The deputy coroner continued telling the jury that there was a bullet hole in the right side of the head of the decedent and that his heart was cut out and removed, pointing at the autopsy pictures.

"That's all I have, if the defense wants to cross examine the coroner he can have at it." Baker responded.

"Oh, just one or two questions." Miller said breezily.

"What happened to the cloths the decedent was wearing?"

The deputy coroner responded "They were folded and placed in a locker at the coroner's office. They are still there."

Baker interrupted "Those cloths are open for the defense to inspect at any time, If the defendant wants I will arrange for such an inspection at any hour of the day and night."

Miller asked "What about the personal possessions? What stuff was in the pockets."

The deputy coroner said, "There was nothing in his pockets or on him except a gold cross with his name on the back and a date of 1930."

"Thank you. No further questions."

Dr. Phillip Baxter was called as a witness. He gave his qualifications as a forensic pathologist and coroner. He stated "I had discovered that the bullet was removed from the skull before the body was found and the fact that his heart was ripped out was the cause of death. The lack of blood means he was butchered somewhere else and wrapped in a plastic sheet and dumped."

The city attorney asked was there anything else? The coroner replied, "Yes it was and they were sloppy."

Mr. Miller asked the coroner "How did you connect my client Miss Alexander with the decedent?"

"We took a hair sample from the defendant and matched it to the hairs we found on the body and we found latex medical gloves with the defendant's right handprint inside and the decedents blood on the out-side." The defense attorney sat down saying no further questions.

It was 2 p.m. when the jury went to discuss the evidence and one hour later they had found enough evidence to bind her over for trial. The judge said to the defendant "Miss Alexander, the inquest jury found enough evidence to hold you for trial on the charge of first-degree murder and desecration of the body. You are to remain in the custody of the county sheriff till January 8, 1949 at 8 a.m. in this courtroom. Deputy Reed removes the defendant, next case."

As she was led out in a waist and hand shackle and leg irons, she gave Officer Younger an evil "I'll see you later look" as she left and as the door closed, he got a cold chill that ran through him, and he shuttered. Corporal Younger made it back to the station at 5 p.m. for his shift and as he left the locker room he ran into Officer Leeds who said "How did court go?"

"Dan! That woman gives me the chills and there is something very evil about her."

They pulled out of the police garage in their patrol car and radioed the dispatcher that they were '10 41, available for service." As they drove down Parkland Drive West, they received a call from dispatch to meet Sergeant Knight at Mayer's Drug Store. As they drove to the drug store Leeds said to Younger "It's tough for Mike, I hope he can stay clean."

"So do I Dan, so do I."

As they pulled up to the drug store they saw Sergeant Knight sitting at a table in the back and as they entered several people greeted the two officers by name and as they approached their fellow cop he said "Hi Peter, Dan."

Both me say "Hi Mike."

Sergeant Knight asked Corporal Younger "How did court go?"

"She was bound over till her January 1949 trial. We still need to find the group leader and who is the deputy sheriff in the group."

Corporal Leeds replied, "Has internal affairs gotten involved yet over this deputy sheriff?"

Sergeant Knight replied "No Dan. The chief and sheriff don't want to tip off the deputy in question.

"Well, how do we investigate this deputy? Won't we tip him off?" Leeds asked.

"No. If we keep it focused on the group and finding its leader whoever it is won't suspect a thing. I suggest we meet for lunch at Danny D's where we can talk without people hearing us, since the jukebox is on so loud." Sergeant Knight said.

In a house across town that has seen better days William Lorax the head of the Temple of Moloch was talking to his high priestess "Lisa. We need to have another sacrifice, child not adult. We need to find an orphan or a kid no one will miss as we need to stay undercover."

Lisa asked, "Does our member in the sheriff's office have anything?"

"No nothing. Since he's not involved in the investigation I told him to avoid appearing too interested in it. He says police Corporals Younger and Leeds are investigating and reporting to Sergeant Knight, Chief Carter and less so to the county sheriff."

It was the evening of November 23$^{rd}$ as Corporal Younger left the locker room and ran into Deputy Sheriff Allen Ellington "Hi Peter."

Looking up Younger said "Oh, Hi Allen. How's it going?"

It's slow the sheriff is still mad you are not filling him in in full about that occult murder."

"Well, that's the chief's doing. I was told discuss this with no one but Sergeant Knight and himself, so if that upsets the sheriff, oh well."

"Well, keep an eye on Officers Lee and Smith. There up to something. I've been getting the smell of dead fish."

"Oh, what gave you that feeling?"

"Well, they seem to have more money than they earn and when I asked them to share they got upset."

"Ok, I'll keep an eye on them."

As the two cops leave the locker room Officers Lee and Smith enter and upon seeing Younger, Officer Lee says "Can we speak to you Peter? It won't be but a second."

Younger looks at Deputy Ellington and says, "Go on ahead, I'll catch up shortly."

As the deputy leaves Younger turns to the pair "What can I do for you two?"

Officer Lee responds "We'd like to see if you would consider earning an extra $400 a week. Nothing criminal, just giving us information on events related to the two of us. Running information checks on people, again nothing wrong or criminal."

"Can I ask why you're approaching me?"

"Well Peter, we know you're a great officer and have an issue with always facing serial killers and our employer wants to pay you for only information and will protect you from serial killers." Officer Smith says.

"Why do I need protection? Do you two know something I don't?" Younger asks in a serious voice.

"No, no we don't. Just thinking on it, that's all." With that both officers leave. Corporal Younger wondered what those two had in mind. He decided to go to his stepfather retired Tillman Police Captain Jimmy Saunders, the only person he could trust with something like this.

He leaves the police station in his unmarked patrol car checking for tails and in ten minutes he's outside his stepfather's house. He parks on the side and gets out and goes and knocks on the door. A voice asks, "Who is it?"

"Captain Saunders, its Corporal Younger. I need to talk to you."

The door opens and a stocky man of 65 years with short grey hair and a cop stance opens the door.

Younger enters the hallway his stepfather closes and locks the door and turns and asks "How are you doing? How is Sally? What's wrong Peter?"

"Sally is doing great and I guess I am ok, Captain Saunders, sort of."

"What do you mean Peter 'sort of? Call me Jimmy."

"Well two cops both reportedly crooked approached me and asked me if I wanted to earn some extra by giving them information that they need; after that they commented on the fact that serial killers seem to find me. They hinted I'd need protection, but said they had no information on any threats and told me to think on it."

"Would the cops be named Lee and Smith?"

"Yes! How did you know?"

"There were rumors when I was on the job that they were for sale and I had my suspicions. Another cop named Paulson was also recruited by them. Didn't you know him before the force?"

"Yes. We served in WW2 together in the military police and graduated from the police academy together. Well, I'm not sure what to do about this; there is no solid proof and I don't want to turn them in as we both know what happens to cops who turn on other cops."

Corporal Younger was referring to three city cops mysteriously killed in 1941 and 1945 on traffic stops when there back up was late. In 1946 another cop was killed by a hit and run driver outside the police station. All four turned in cops for corruption.

"Well Peter, you can tell them no and you two do that you want, but leave me out of it, or you can join them and sell your soul, but either way it's up to you. I'm going to stay out of this because I am no longer a cop and I'll just make things worse if I step in."

Monday, November 24, 1948 was a bad day for Corporal Younger. He was called into the chief's office and told of the death of Officer Rodger Paulson who was found in his squad car on Parkland Dive East at the coroner of seventeenth street; he was shot twice in the head and was found by two people out for a walk. It was 9 p.m. last night when I got the call from Sheriff Davids and went out there."

The chief continued "The sheriff offered his whole department to help catch his killer. The state patrol also offered its help." Corporal

Younger sat down and started to cry. He and Paulson graduated from the police academy together, both served in the same military police unit in WW2 and Younger was dating his older sister.

The chief said 'The sheriff's department was taking point in the homicide investigation, so it can be untainted when they finally catch the killers. Rumors also say it was two fellow city cops that did it."

"Chief, could the cult have done it? I mean he was helping me investigate them."

"No Peter. The scene showed he knew or was comfortable with the killer or killers, and if it was one of the cult you'd be a prime target as your running the investigation and he had no direct role. The funeral will be held at Baker's Funeral Home on December 5$^{th}$ at 10 a.m."

Officer Younger leaves the police station and signs out and heads for Dot's Coroner Bar. He arrives and sits at the bar and orders several whiskeys straight and starts drinking. The bartender who knows Younger and why he's drinking since it's a cop bar; after giving him his condolences he goes and calls Sergeant Knight.

Ten minutes later Sergeant Knight enters and goes over to Younger and sits down and asks for a coke. He turns too Younger and says "Look Peter, I know you two were close, but drinking like a fish doesn't help take it from me. Alcohol makes it worse. Leave your car here and go upstairs to one of the rooms Phil uses for cops who had too much to drink, your very drunk." With that Sergeant Knight and Phil, the bartender helps Younger up to room 7 dump him on the bed and leave. Phil locks the door and takes Youngers car keys. At 10 a.m. Sergeant Knight unlocks the door opens it to find Younger dressed after a shower drinking coffee, and sitting with him was Miss Pattched sitting next to him hair also damp which means they spent the night together.

Sergeant Knight says as he enters "Peter! What is Miss Pattched doing here? How did she get in?"

Miss Pattched replied "Sergeant Knight, I knew Corporal Younger was attracted to me and wanted to fuck my brains out, but he wasn't ready. I found out what happened, where he was and came over and as for how I got in, let's say I had some help which you would not believe."

Corporal Younger looks at her and his mind drifts back to how she found him. He vaguely remembers the bartender and Knight helping him into the room.

He was awakened by a presence in the room and she stood there wearing crotch less panties and a silk nighty and silk gloves and she walked towards him saying "Let me help you, I know you want to fuck me and I want to fuck you raw."

Next thing he knew he was naked with her sitting on the edge of the bed caressing his face as she kissed him full on the mouth with her pink full wet lips and she instinctively curled her tongue around his. She then let him feel her beautifully formed firm breasts and as he cupped her breasts and he slowly sucked on them as she moaned, and they got firmer and she slid her gloved hand to his penis.

Her gloved hands tightened even more around his straining shaft and her lips massaged the hot smooth column of flesh between her fingers, then she leaned down and began licking the swollen head as his cock had bloomed into a thick swollen masterpiece. She sucked him and as she sucked harder, he moaned and her tongue slid up and down and after one hour he exploded in her mouth and she loved the feel of his cock deep in her mouth as she swallowed his salty cum and he lost it and she sucked him dry.

"That was wonderful." He said under his breath.

"You haven't felt nothing yet Peter." She said as she licked her wet lips.

She then sat her luscious, silky, wet pussy over his mouth. As he kissed the moist warm folds between her thighs she allowed his tongue to go deep into pussy where she wanted fulfillment.

As his tongue worked in and out her pink womanly center pulsated and tingled with pleasure as she had an orgasm, and he drank her cum and found her g-spot. She then took his penis into her slippery wet pussy, and she continued the slow and steady motion, sliding up and down his engorged flesh and soon she fucked all the cum out of him while he begged for her to stop, but she refused.

Her eyes went from azure to coal black as she had several orgasms and her cruel, hungry eyes said 'your mine'. He lost track of time and soon the alarm truck 6 a.m. and he was surprised to see her on top of him and she simply said, "Good morning, Peter, you were excellent, and your penis is mine."

"I never knew you wanted me that much, and why did you show up and how did you get in?" He asked.

She replied "My spirit followed you and watched and saw you needed and wanted a woman and I came here and he opened the door, locked it and I sexually fucked all the cum out of you. I am clean and won't get pregnant. They got up and took a shower together and got dressed and were eating breakfast when Sergeant Knight opened the door.

"Peter how did Miss Pattched get in? I had the key and the door locked."

She replied "Sergeant Knight, you wouldn't believe it, so just accept this. I'll see you later Peter."

As she left Peter said "Mike. I still don't believe her explanation of how she got in, nor do I want to know."

"Well, don't worry about it Peter. She just freaks me out."

They leave and head to the police station. As they entered the police station, they ran into Deputy Chief Allen Liebermann and Vice Detective Bill Edwards.

Younger says "Morning Deputy Chief Liebermann, Detective Edwards."

Deputy Chief Liebermann replies "Morning Peter, Mike. Any progress on the murder of Officer Paulson?"

"No deputy chief, were just about to start om it. We also have to continue investigating the cult murders." Younger replied.

"Well, let me know if you need any of my men to help in both cases." Vice Detective Edwards replied.

Younger and Knight headed to the locker room to get into uniform. As they got dressed Corporal Younger opened his locker and an 11 by 17 envelope fell to the floor and it had his name on it. He picked it up and opened it and inside was a picture of Officer Lee and Smith accepting a payoff from a local mobster/drug dealer with writing on the back '7/12/1942 Parkland Park East'. Corporal Younger showed Sergeant Knight the picture and says, "We got them!"

Sergeant Knight thought for a second then said, "Wait one second Peter. We need more than one photograph, we need to catch them in the act and we need more evidence. But we should show this to the chief; just don't tell Lee and Smith you have this, you may just get killed."

The two officers while walking to the chief's office see Officers Lee and Smith talking to Lieutenant Parker from internal affairs and an envelope changes hands. The two officers don't see Younger and Knight and leave. Knight looks at Younger and says, "Well that leaves out internal affairs."

The chief after listening to his two officers telling him the facts and Younger tells him and shows him the picture he received and looking at the picture says, "Corporal Younger! What do you and Sergeant Knight mean?" Younger thinks a second before speaking, "Well chief, Officers Lee and Smith are corrupt and now we see them handling Lieutenant Parker from internal Affairs an envelope."

The chief replies, "This confirms what I suspected about Lee and Smith and Parker. Do you believe Lee and Smith killed Officer Paulson?"

"Yes chief, at least Officer Lee as this is the bullet taken from Officer Paulson and a bullet from Officer Lee's gun from the gun range target and the state crime lab says they are a match 97.5%, we just need his gun." Younger replies.

Sergeant Knight asks the chief, "Do we go to Bob Baker, the city attorney and tell him what's going on and ask if we arrest them?"

"Before you do that, let me talk to Lieutenant Parker and force him to choose sides."

"Are you going to be safe chief doing this?" Sergeant Knight asks.

"Yes, I will be sergeant. I know Parker and he's a good man and I'll be safe."

The chief knows Lieutenant Parker eats lunch in his car parked at West Fifth Street near the fountain. Ten minutes later the chief pulls his car up behind Parker's gets out and opens the passenger door and got in and said, "Afternoon Lieutenant Parker."

Parker looks up saying, "Afternoon chief. What do I owe the pleasure of this visit?"

"I have an update on the murder of Officer Paulson and this needs your unit as it involves another cop."

"Who's the suspected cop? And what proof do you have? This is a serious issue and if you pull the trigger on this, you better have proof."

"Well, I have the bullet taken from Officer Paulson's head and the bullet taken from the shooting range target, witnesses statement of the cop in Paulson's patrol car in the right side back seat. All I need is the officer's gun and it's a closed case with 100% conviction. We don't need a cop who kill other cops among us."

"Who's the cop?" Does the city attorney know? What do you need from me and my men?"

"Well, err first I need to know if I can trust you as besides you, me, the city attorney and the two cops who cracked the case no one else knows. We don't need more cops killed either directly or indirectly."

"Look chief. I know people have questions if I would take down another cop and I also know about the event in 1944 that also makes people question me and my dedication."

"Well Parker, you were seen with the cop in question and his partner being handed an envelope and the officer said to you *don't blow this Parker.*"

Parker suddenly knows it's either Officer Lee or Smith who killed Paulson or both and that this was dangerous. He also knows the chief knows, so all he says is "SHIT!"

The chief looked at his lieutenant and said. "You look like someone walked over your grave Parker. You can go after the cop who killed Paulson and nothing else you did or have done needs to come out."

"OK chief, who is it?"

"Officer Lee. The witness said he heard them arguing and Lee telling Paulson I hate you and you're a Judas and I don't need a reason to hate you and do this. That's when Lee kills Paulson."

They sit in the car in silence for ten minutes. Lieutenant Parker says, "Chief! Your right I can arrest Lee and other stuff won't come out, are you sure?"

"Yes Parker. I want Lee because he killed Paulson without reason, which means we cops can't trust him. If he feels another cop is a threat he could kill again. I don't care what the envelope contained. I want a killer cop before he kills another cop again. He made a threat against Corporal Younger last week."

"Well chief let's get three of my men, you get Younger and Knight and we go get Officer Lee. His partner Officer Smith as long as he isn't implicated won't have a problem dumping Lee. What will the other cops think? Cops who go after other cops don't have a long life or career."

"Parker! We'll arrest Officer Lee in the police locker room at shift change and announce he's under arrest for the capital murder of Officer Paulson and I'll ask him why did you kill him? What did he do to deserve to die? Are there any other cops you plan to kill? The other cops want whoever murdered Paulson, so let's do this before we get cold feet."

# Chapter Three

So, on the morning of December 15, 1948 Chief Carter, Internal Affairs Lieutenant Parker with three of his men along with Corporal Younger and Sergeant Knight with the warrant in hand entered the full police locker room and approached Officer Lee and Lieutenant Parker says, "Officer Lee I have a warrant for your arrest for the capital murder of Officer Paulson." As two of Parker's men handcuffed him, Chief Carter steps up, "Damn it, Lee! What did Paulson do to deserve to be killed by you? Did you hate him that much? Why did you blow his brains out? We have hard evidence of your cold-blooded act, why damn it."

The locker room is silent as all the other cops look at Officer Lee and Corporal Younger says, "Last week you threatened to kill me! What did I do to warrant that? Was I next on your list?"

As Officer Lee was led out he said nothing and the other cops when asked by the chief bluntly they all said Officer Lee was on his own, even Officer Smith agreed.

The afternoon of December 15th Officer Lee in a black and white jail jumper appears before Judge Carrel Kingsley who after the court clerk says, "The city of Tillman, Nebraska versus Officer Charles Lee case 48-736425 one count capital murder of Tillman Police Officer Rodger Paulson." The judge says, "how does the defendant pled?"

Officer Lee replies, "Not Guilty your honor."

The city attorney Bob Baker playing to the voters asks the judge, "We request remand your honor as he poses a threat to other cops; he threatened to kill Corporal Younger last week."

The judge looked at Officer Lee and simply says, "The defendant will be held in the city jail till his trial at 8 a.m. January 17, 1949 in this court room. Court officer remove the defendant."

As the court officer led Officer Lee out of the court room he suddenly moves to the court officer and takes his gun and as he starts to raise it towards Corporal Younger and City Attorney Bob Baker it is like in slow motion and Sergeant Knight pulls his gun and shoots Officer Lee dead. The court room is cleared. The judge looks at Sergeant Knight and says, "Don't worry your shooting was justified."

Officer Smith walks up to Corporal Younger and says, "Sorry Peter about what Lee did. I was scared if I tried to stop him I'd have been killed next."

"Don't worry about it Officer Smith what's done is done and I have no intention of looking into anything you've done that's up to internal affairs. You have nothing to fear from me."

"Thanks Corporal Younger. I'm glad this is over. The other officers won't do anything to you, Officer Lee did this to himself."

Corporal Younger and Sergeant Knight left the courthouse and headed back to police headquarters to inform Chief Carter of what just happened. Suddenly Corporal Younger looks at his patrol car and yells, "WHAT THE FUCK! There is an inverted pentagram in blood on the hood of my car."

Sergeant Knight, City Attorney Baker, and Sheriff Davids run over and the sheriff stares in disbelief at the hood of the car.

Corporal Younger knows this as a threat and he sees two newspaper reporters and calls them over and says take this down word for word. "Gentleman the cult fuckers who painted this on my car will go down. I and the police will not be intimidated. You just gave me another reason to end your terror. You cultists will go down either by court or bullet. You reporters take that word for word and pictures."

One of the reporters asks Corporal Younger, "Aren't you scared to threaten these cult murders? Don't you think it will make you a target?"

"NO! Killing a cop will bring down every state, local cop on their ass and they will be hunted, not even they would be that stupid."

Across town the founder of the Church of Moloch was sitting with his high priestess and two other cult members and slams the local paper down and yells, "Who the hell decided to threaten a cop with death? Before this was a straight murder investigation, now we have death threats against a cop who has nothing. Why give him a reason to increase the search for us."

His high priestess Lisa Planetello tells the other two church members, "Find out who the idiot was who did this and let me know, this calls for discipline."

Both men say together, "Yes high priestess."

The high priest tells his second, "Tell the others stay away from the cops unless I tell them otherwise, understand?"

"Yes, I do." She simply says as she leaves. The two church members were waiting for her and one of them asks, "Priestess what do we do when we find the person who did this?"

"Bring them to me and when I see who it is, I'll make a decision. But everyone stays away from the cops unless the high priest says different."

Corporal Younger on the evening of December 15^th got a visit from Miss Pattached who walked into the squad room and walked up to Corporal Younger's desk and said, "Hello Peter. I heard what happened."

"Yes, Leslie they got serious. Well even psychos will not harm police, they don't strike me as crazy enough to threaten cops."

"Well, that may be so Peter, but you're hunting them and the closer you get the more risk you will be under. My spirits tell me that those people are wanting to avoid confrontation, but their power is such that my spirits can't find them. They say those cultists have some powerful powers available."

"Well don't worry Leslie. I'm careful to always check my surroundings and watch for tails, so I'm not worried."

"Well Peter. I came by to see if you were available tonight for some dinner and sex, are you?"

"Yes Leslie. My shift ends at 9 p.m. in about thirty minutes. I'll meet you at your place."

Leslie says in a seductive voice, "See you then Peter and be prepared for the fuck of your life." With that she leaves and Sergeant Knight looks at Peter and says, "You going to be able to walk tomorrow?"

"Why do you say that Mike?"

"I've seen the look she gives you and she looks like she can fuck a man to death."

"Yes, she can and what a way to go. I'm sure I am safe, see you tomorrow morning." Corporal Younger leaves the locker room in his civilian cloths and his 9mm gun under his right arm as he walks to his car. He gets in and notices nothing strange and heads to Leslie's house. He then remembers his main girlfriend Sally will be back from California in three weeks and he needs to tell Leslie about her, so as no cat-fights happen.

He pulls up to her apartment parks and gets out. He felt eyes on him and he stopped and stood for four minutes outside slowly looking around. He didn't see anyone, but he felt it was just keeping tabs on him and did not want to have contact. He shrugged then entered Leslie's building and walked up to the third floor, preparing himself to get fucked without mercy. He knocked on her door and her voice asked, "Who is it?"

"It's Peter, Leslie."

The door opened and she appeared in a see through blue silk nighty with matching gloves and she said, "Come on in Peter I've been waiting for you." He entered and saw her close the door locks it and put on the chain. She walked to the bar and made two Jack and cokes on ice and they sat down and had drinks and dinner. Younger then said, "What do you have in mind Leslie?"

"Well, I'm going to strip you naked tie you spread eagle on the bed and fuck and suck you till you beg. I'm horny, wet and want you."

She helped him strip and he put his gun on the nightstand and once naked she tied him loosely with the rope so he could get out if needed. She climbed on top of him and started deep French kissing him. Her eyes were hungry and lust filled as she devoured his mouth with deep sweeping strokes of her tongue and she drew his tongue into her mouth. Their tongues danced as each of their bodies melted together in this sacred union. He felt her full hot pink lips as they kissed. They kissed as he felt her warm silk gloved hands slowly roaming over his chest.

Then about ten minutes later she sat her hot, warm, silky pussy over his mouth and his tongue entered deep into her moist warm pussy and his tongue worked too free her delicious nectar as her mouth, lips and tongue moved up and down his iron hard cock while her silky gloved hands massaged the hot, smooth column of flesh between her silk fingers then she began licking the swollen head. For what was about an hour they did the 69 position till they both climaxed at the same time and they both swallowed. She climbed off and said, "Your great as ever at eating my pussy.

"Well Leslie, you're getting better at finding ways to suck all the cum out of me." With that she takes his hard dick in her hands and quivers as it enters the tight depths of her receptive pussy and she rode him like a bronco missionary style as he strained against the restraints as her silky hands skimmed his chest as his breath got harsher and they both felt the orgasm coming with a burst of pleasure he came deep in her and she shuddered as her cum exploded out and ran down his cock.

The wet feeling made them both groan and she collapsed on him breathing heavy and they laid there for thirty minutes and she said simply, "I want to ride you some more." So, she rode him for another four hours and they fell asleep. Sometime in the night she untied him. Her alarm clock went off at 8 a.m. on that cold December morning of the sixteenth and after they showered and ate breakfast he told her he'd see her tonight as he had to report for duty in one hour. Before he left he said' "Leslie, my main girl Sally will be back in three weeks and we'll need to slow this down. She doesn't like three ways."

Leslie looked at him and said, "I'll fight her for you." Then she just laughed and added, "Just kidding Peter. I believe we can work it out and she might surprise you, wouldn't you like to fuck both of us at the same time?"

He thought for a second and finally said, "Yes I would, but not at the risk of losing her and causing her pain."


Corporal Jim Andrews of the Nebraska State Patrol was driving his patrol car down Parkland Drive West towards Central Boulevard when he suddenly heard a loud scream. He stopped his car and tried to find out where it came from. He then noticed a naked bleeding blond woman running towards him screaming "HELP ME PLEASE! HELP ME THERE TRYING TO KILL ME."

There were two men in dark robes chasing her with large knives and he got out. He helped the woman get behind his car and called for assistance. "State patrol car 11, need backup corner of Seventh Avenue and Parkland Drive West, two men with knives."

The dispatcher said, "Rodger state car 11. All available Tillman units code 10-39 officer needs assistance, coroner Seventh Avenue and Parkland Drive West, handle code 3." At that point four Tillman cars responded.

He yelled at the men, "STOP WHERE YOU ARE! DROP THE KNIVES AND GET DOWN ON THE GROUND." The men kept advancing, so he pulled his pistol and shot both men dead. At that moment four Tillman Black and whites and a state car pulled up skidding to a stop.

As the trooper turned to the woman a shot rings out and the back of the woman's head explode as a Tillman cops bullet hit her. The cop who fired the shot yells, "Look in her hands, look in her hands." He looked and she held a large butcher knife.

He thought where did she get the knife? She's naked. Lieutenant Parker of the Tillman Internal Affairs walks up saying, "Trooper. You, ok?"

"Yes, Lieutenant Parker I am. I just wasn't expecting this." Another Tillman cop Officer Samuel Hood approaches the woman's body and says, "Shit! That's my missing sister!"

Lieutenant Parker exclaims, "What do you mean missing Officer Hood?"

"My older sister vanished three weeks ago and I've been looking for her. Why would she have a knife and try to kill a cop? She was never violent and what about those two men?"

The coroner looking the men over notices a tattoo of Moloch on each man's arm. "Lieutenant Parker, will you come here please?"

"What is it, Tom?"

"These men are members of the Church of Moloch; isn't that the group Corporal Younger is investigating?"

"Yes, it is. Let me call him over. Corporal Younger will you come here please?"

Walking over Corporal Younger with Corporal Leeds asks his lieutenant, "What's up?"

"These two men tried to kill that woman and were killed by Trooper Andrews. They were members of the Church of Moloch."

"Who's the dead woman?" Corporal Leeds asks.

"Officer Hoods missing older sister. Somehow she joined the church." Lieutenant Parker replied.

Corporal Younger tells Officer Hood, "I'll look into your sister to see if I can find out what happened and how she got involved with this cult."

"Peter. I want to join the investigation to find out what happened,"

"OK. You can fill me in on your sister and what she was like." With that Officer Hood heads back to his car and partner and left. Corporal Younger headed back to the station. As he starts his car he gets the feeling of being watched. He looks around and sees a figure under a streetlight one block south watching what was unfolding and then it vanished. Younger wondered was that someone or something from the cult?

On his way back to the station he got a call about a dead body at St. Luke's Church. He shook his head grimly as Leeds acknowledged the call and Younger wheeled his black and white cruiser in a tight circle of the block, reversing directions.

Younger found the church and swung his vehicle curbside behind one of the four black and whites at the scene. A young patrolman was crossing the lawn toward the black and whites. The cop gave Younger and Leeds directions to a brick path that led them alongside the church to a Northside entrance that another cop stood at and he passed him entering.

The corridor beyond filled with the confusion which follows murder like flies following a garbage truck. Several policemen were in evidence accompanied by the usual crew of crime lab people, photographer, newspapermen and the ambulance attendants who would take the victim one last ride to the morgue. It was a familiar scene too Corporal Younger and Leeds and it no longer depressed them.

They brushed through the milling throng homing as much by instinct as by sight on the sources of that hubbub as he entered the chapel door he recognized, Sergeant Mike Knight, among the four men standing at the altar, but paused before approaching them, his eyes surveying the havoc which had been wreaked upon the austere room.

Younger was no stranger to vandalism having witnessed it in every form during his years on the force. This somehow struck him differently. It was pointed somehow bearing a message of some indecipherable import too the vandals more than anything else; it put Younger in mind of a case he had handled and broken while a patrolman involving a group of teenaged self-styled anarchists who spent their evenings vandalizing Jewish graves. There was the same twisted, ghoulish aura about the vandalism before him now.

Younger shrugged the moment aside and joined the men around the altar. Knight nodded a grim and silent greeting stepping back to permit Younger and Leeds an unobstructed view of what lay upon that altar.

The nude body of a young woman lay before him. She was blond and young. Younger placed her age roughly between nineteen and twenty-one. She had been pretty once, her face and body presenting an image of almost beauty that was coming among second string starlets and small-time nightclub singers.

In death she was pale and stiff, eyes closed an expression of uncommon composure on her lifeless face. The girl had died violently, Younger's eyes traveled from the long gash across her soft white throat to the single blood encrusted stab wound between her round breasts, pausing then to linger over the strange colored designs which had been painted upon her abdomen and thighs painted before death he observed, since the welling blood from the throat and chest wounds had overlapped and obscured the ritualistic designs in some places.

Strangely, for one who has met a most violent death at such an age, the girl looked peaceful. There was no sign to indicate that she had resisted her murders in any way in fact her pose was one of total ease and relaxation as if she had known full well what she was about to suffer and had not only recognized but welcomed it. The coroners of her dark lips turned upward slightly, in a vague little Cheshire cat smile.

"It's an odd one Peter." Mike Knight said over his shoulder giving voice to Younger's own thoughts. Younger nodded mute assent.

Sergeant Knight led Younger back into the access corridor behind the altar where they found an aging priest and another old man facing rapid-fire questions from a trio of newsmen. Younger brushed through the ranks of the press, shepherding the two witnesses toward a tiny office that opened off the corridor.

"Give the city a chance okay?" He snapped as he swept past the fuming newspapermen. Leaving Knight to close the door firmly behind them the sergeant joined them quickly, introducing Younger and Leeds to Father John Garner and George Kronoski, the church caretaker. Younger started his questioning with Kronoski.

"You found the body this morning?" He knew the answer already but had to break the ice somehow with the nervous Oldman.

Kronoski nodded briskly, obviously agitated as he rasped, "Yes sir."

"Did you see anyone or anything unusual around the church? Outside I mean?"

A brisk negative headshake, "NO. Nobody here but me when I come."

"And you didn't touch or move anything inside?"

Again, the headshake, "NO sir, no."

Younger turned his attention to the priest, a nagging hunch telling him the old man had more to say.

"When did you arrive, father Garner?"

"About fifteen minutes ago," The white-haired priest replied. "George was frightened so he called me first. I called the police from my home, then came directly over here."

Younger nodded. He tried a longshot. "Did you see the body father?"

"Yes. It's terrible the poor child."

"Have you ever seen her before? Perhaps here in church?"

The padre immediately shook his head. "No. I've thought about that already. I've never seen the poor child before in my life."

Younger sighed his longshot had come up empty, and he tried a different tack, "Do you or the church have any particular enemies in the neighborhood, father?"

The priest looked confused, "Enemies? Why I don't— "

"Irate parishioners? Maybe an atheistic neighbor who seems a little odd?"

Father Garner shook his head sternly. "Absolutely not. I cannot believe any of our parishioners or neighbors are responsible for this blasphemy."

Younger nodded hopelessly, getting nowhere fast. "I noticed some candles on the altar, father are they..." He never got to finish the question, for the mention of those black candles seemed to throw the old caretaker into a fit of agitation. He wrung his hands, muttering under his breath as he rocked from foot to foot. Younger could make out nothing that he said beyond some muttered words and phrases in what sounded like a foreign language. The priest moved quickly, placing a comforting arm about the caretaker's shoulders and speaking to him softly, soothingly.

"He is frightened," Garner explained when he turned back toward Younger and Knight after a long moment. "He believes the murder to have some association with devil worship."

Mike Knight's voice was filled with incredulity, "Devil worship? Aw, c'mon father."

Younger was matter of fact and to the point, "What do you think, father?"

The padre shrugged, "Those candles do bear certain resemblance to the ones used in a black mass, that is. I believe that some like them are sold at novelty shops in the state. Some people take the old satanic rituals quite seriously I'm told, but to sacrifice another human being, though not so emphatically this time. This I cannot believe."

Corporal Peter Younger thanked the padre and left the tiny office, Knight and Leeds trailing behind him. The sergeant's voice brought Younger up short. "Say Peter, this sounds like the Church of Moloch."

# Chapter Four

Corporal Peter Younger on the morning of December 20<sup>th</sup> went to the bus station to pick up his girl Sally who was coming back from her California trip to see her brother and sister. As he stood beside his patrol car he wondered how he was going to explain Leslie to her.

The bus from California arrived exactly at 10:30 a.m. and he saw Sally get off the bus. He runs over to her saying, "Sally, I missed you, welcome home." Sally turns and they embrace kissing each other and she says, "It's great to be home again."

"How is your brother Phil and your sister Mary?"

"They are fine Peter, and they miss you just not the cold weather." As he picks up her bags and walk to his patrol car she looks at him and asks, "Who is Leslie?"

Peter thinks to himself how do I answer this? But he replies, "She is a police witness and adviser of the occult helping us to solve a case."

"There isn't anything else going on, like sex?"

"I was going to mention that to you. How did you find out?"

"I received a letter from my best friend Benny who mentioned it in passing."

"Well now that you know, but I did tell Leslie that when you came back it all ends, the sex part that is."

"Did she agree to it? You know I don't like to share."

"Yes, she did, but she did offer to make it a threesome."

"I am not sure Peter that I would like that very much."

"OK, let's get you home then as I got to get back to work. I get off at 9:30 p.m. and I'll come by."

They pulled up to Corporal Youngers house and he helped her take her bags inside and kissed her as he left saying, "I'll see you tonight"

He drives back to the station and as he walks past the desk sergeants desk he says, "Corporal Younger the chief wants to see you. He's meeting with the sheriff in his office."

Younger heads to the chief's office and knocks on the door and a voice asks, "Who is it?"

"Chief, its Corporal Younger."

Come in Younger."

Younger opens the door and sees the sheriff and says, "Morning chief, Sheriff Davids."

"Morning Corporal Younger." The sheriff replies.

"What did you want to see me about chief?"

"Those two men the state trooper killed and the girl one of our men killed had tattoos on the underside of their arms of the Church of Moloch, is that right?"

"Yes, it is. Here is a picture of the three people with the tattoos." Younger put the pictures on the desk for the sheriff and chief to see. "Were keeping this under wraps as there is a rumor a deputy sheriff is a member, and we don't want to tip anyone off." Corporal Younger sits down waiting to see if there were any questions.

The sheriff asks Younger, "Corporal what are you going to do when you find the deputy sheriff who's a member of this cult?"

"Well sheriff; I'll inform you; Chief Carter and I'll keep it quiet so I can maybe be led to the cults location. I'll let our internal affairs and yours know also."

"You're not going to let the city attorney know?"

"No sheriff I'm not. It's way too early to tell him, besides I want an open and shut case that sticks." As the meeting broke up he looked at his watch and saw it was 9 p.m. so he headed to the squad room to do some paperwork, then at 9:30 p.m. he signed out and went home.

It took him five minutes to get home to his house and he parked in the drive way got out and seeing Leslie's car he unlocked the door and entered entering the living room when Sally came out hugged and kissed him and she took his hand and led him to the living room. He entered the living room and saw Leslie Pattchard sitting on the couch and before he could say something she spoke up. "I know how this looks Peter. I had to meet Sally, don't be mad."

"Leslie, I thought I mentioned this that I would tell Sally about you and explain. Why did you come over to see her?"

"I thought I could explain things better as a woman and it would be a woman to woman exchange."

Sally looked at Peter and replied, "Yes Peter she did come over and explained things and she explained how she drew you in and explained why."

"Why was that, Leslie?"

"Well Peter one of my spirit guides told me that the cult you are investigating wanted to recruit you in. They were going to get you to have sex with a female cult member and blackmail you into joining or force you to stop investigating them. I decided to step in to prevent their plans also I was attracted to you."

"So, what now? I'm in love with Sally and intend to spend the rest of my life with her. How is this going to work?"

Sally spoke up, "Well Peter I decided that the three of us will have group sex and me and Leslie will please you, and you can please both of us."

After thinking on it for five minutes he replied, "Are you sure Sally? I love you and only you and don't want this to affect our relationship."

"Well don't worry Peter this is not going to affect us and Leslie will leave the relationship with no problem."

Leslie replied, "Yes Peter when the time comes I will depart gracefully and there will be no hard feelings."

With that they went into the kitchen and ate a late dinner. Sally asked, "Peter do you have to work tomorrow?"

"No Sally I'm off unless an emergency comes up why?"

"Well Peter when I asked Leslie about this threesome I asked what did she and you like to do and how. She explained the two of you did the usual missionary sex along with what she calls the 69 position and how she got you turned on by wearing gloves and tying you down to the bed and fucking and sucking you dry. I never knew you were into that."

"I wasn't till I met Leslie and it was not exactly as I asked for it, she just did it."

It was 10:30 p.m. when Leslie said, "How about me, you and Sally go upstairs to your bedroom and I show her how you like it and how fun it is to reverse gangbang a restrained man."

Inside Peter was scared as he knew Sally was a nympho and Leslie was a super nympho, but he was turned on as the two women he loved were going to make his night.

They entered the master bedroom and Leslie put a bag on the nightstand and told him, "Get naked Peter and I'll teach Sally how you like it."

He was nervous as he took his equipment belt off then all his cloths and by time he was naked Leslie and Sally were also nude and Leslie told him, "Lay on your back and spread your arms and legs."

He then laid on the bed spread-eagle and Leslie produced four rope restraints and told Sally, "You tie his hands to the headboard and I'll do his legs."

After they had him restrained Leslie went back into the bag and produced two pairs of latex rubber exam gloves and gave one pair to Sally and they both put them on and climbed on the bed on either side and started running their gloved hands over his body. Both women kissing him and they let him suck both their breasts. Then the two women started kissing each othet.

He saw both women quiver with pleasure and Leslie said, "Before you came home me and Sally pleasured each other and I showed her stuff she loved." Then both women took their gloved hands and stroked his iron hard cock and both women ran their tongues up and down and both used their lips on the head of his penis and the feeling of latex gloves with both women's warm mouth and tongues got him harder and he strained against the restraints as both women picked up the pace and after enduring fifty-five minutes he came and both women shared his hot sperm and swallowed it all with Leslie finishing it. With that Leslie sits her pussy over his mouth and as he eats her silky, warm pussy making her moan and have an explosive organism as Sally got a second load of sperm out, then Leslie said, "Let's switch Sally."

With that Leslie climbed off and Sally sat her blond pussy over his mouth and Peter thought to himself why didn't we do this before?

As he ate Sally's pussy he felt Leslie missionary fucking him hard and Sally came as he filled Leslie's pussy. Sally then climbed off and started fucking him as Leslie used a strap on his ass anally fucking him as Sally rode him. Then every hour they switched and then with Sally on top of him and Leslie on his right side they untied him and they fell asleep.

At 9:30 a.m. on December 21$^{st}$ Sally woke up and rolled off him and said, "Morning Peter that was incredible."

Leslie as she climbed on his morning hard dick that she held in one gloved hand and slid his dick into her, "Yes Peter that was wonderful, how did you like it?"

"Well Leslie, I knew Sally was a nympho but I never knew she was a sexual psycho like you, it was excellent."

"Well glad you liked it." Then she fucked him some more and she and Sally fucked him for two more hours then they all took a shower together, got dressed and ate breakfast. Sally asked what will we do to-day?"

Leslie replied, "Well I have to open my store at 11 a.m., but I'll be buy by seven if that's ok?"

"Yes, Leslie it will be. Me and Sally will be waiting." Sally replied. With that Leslie got up kissed peter and Sally and left.

After she was gone Sally sat down and said, "Peter you ain't mad that me and Leslie did each other and then you?"

"No Sally. I never knew you were bi-sexual and liked that type of sex. I know you were a nympho, but never you liked orgies."

"Well till I met Leslie I never had a three-way and never did another woman. She gave me pleasure I never knew and I wanted and I wanted the three of us to have sex together so it would prevent any jealously issues."

"Well Sally, I never knew you had such an interest in this type of sex."

"Well Peter neither did I till now. I feel this will help all three of us."

"Well let's spend the day out I believe you wanted to go to several antique shops in town."

They got into Peter's car and left to go to the antique shops. They visited Sammy's Antique House, Bill and Jill's Antique emporium, The Antique Warehouse and Susan's Boutique. By 1 p.m. Sally purchased a dressing table with mirror from 1870, several 19th century chairs, and a doll from 1880 and Peter purchased an old Tillman City Police badge and a full uniform (the Tillman City Police existed from 1853-1896 when it was formed into the Tillman Police Department).

They ate lunch as the A&W Root Beer Shop on West Sixth Street and took their purchases home. For the rest of the day they sat at home and had a BBQ with several Tillman cops and their wives in the backyard, there were also two deputy sheriffs there.

When the BBQ ended and everyone left Sally and Peter cleaned up and went in to watch Tillman's only one of two TV channels. At 8:30 p.m. Leslie came over and by 10 p.m. all three were in bed asleep after having sex.

The morning of the 23rd of December it snowed overnight and there was about an inch of snow and the temperature was 24 degrees and cold. They sat around the table eating breakfast and Leslie spoke up, "What are you two doing for Christmas?"

Peter replied, "Well I'll be working the second watch till 8 p.m. and if there are no emergencies time with both of you. Then on Christmas day I'll have to work second watch again."

Sally replied, "Me and Leslie will finish setting up the Christmas tree and get the gifts ready and were having Christmas party."

"Yes, we will. Several fellow officers and their wives and kids will be here including the sheriff, Chief Carter, the mayor and city attorney and several deputy sheriff's" Peter responded.

"Well ladies I have to go on duty three hours early and I hope I'll be home before 10 p.m., but you never know." Peter replied as he put on his police winter coat over his uniform and equipment belt and he left for work. He got into his 1946 Ford patrol car and started it up and picked up his microphone and said, "Car 20 Corporal Younger code 10-41."

The dispatcher replied, "Rodger car 26 your 10-41. The chief wants you to go to the station to meet him."

"Rodger dispatch, eta seven minutes."

As he parked his car and walks to the front door of the police head-quarters the door opens and the sheriff exists angry, "Morning Sheriff Davids."

"Morning Corporal Younger, the chief wants to see you now. That man pisses me off." The sheriff gets into his car and starts the engine and drives off. Corporal Younger wondered what is going on. He enters and walks past the duty desk and climbed the stairs to the second-floor office of the chief.

He knocks on the door and the voice asks, "Who is it?"

"It's Corporal Younger chief, you wanted to see men?"

"Yes, I did Get in here."

Corporal Younger opens the door enters and sees Assistant Chief of Police Liebermann looking grave. "Morning Assistant Chief Liebermann, chief what do you need?"

The chief says, "Well Corporal Younger a young woman walked into the sheriff's office and told the sheriff that a sheriff's deputy tried to assault her and he had a tattoo that resembled the cult ones. She couldn't give a description as he got her from behind and wrestled her into an alley. She did recognize the sheriff's uniform and a badge with the partial number 436."

"The sheriff's badges start with 436 except for Sheriff Davids. Could see she the other numbers?" Younger asks.

"No, she didn't. The sheriff is mad as there are seventy-three possible deputy sheriffs who could be the attacker. If the attacker finds out she can identify him she's dead and if she told anyone else their also dead." The chief said.

The assistant chief says, "Well chief, me and Corporal Younger can investigate as I have access to the sheriff department rosters from 1938 till now and even the sheriff don't know I have them. WE can make a list of the suspects and investigate with on one being the wiser."

"You and Corporal Younger do that asap. I want to know who this deputy is and put him under surveillance." The chief replied.

Both men got up and replied, "Will do chief." Both men left and once outside the chief's office Corporal Younger turned to the assistant chief and said, "Are you serious Allen about this?"

The assistant chief looks at Younger and replies, "Yes I am Peter, very serious."

The two men walk to the squad room and run into Sergeant Knight. Younger says, "Morning Mike."

"Morning Peter, assistant chief what's up?" He asks after seeing the grave look on their faces.

"We may have a way to discover who the cults inside man in the sheriff's department is and the sheriff is not happy about that. Allen has the roster of the sheriff deputies 1938 till now with names and badge numbers. We have a partial badge number. We're going to make a list and secretly investigate them."

# Chapter 5

It was the morning of Christmas eve and the snow covered the ground and since the roads were slick Corporal Younger and Leeds handled ten car accidents before 1 p.m. As they sat in Danny D's eating and doing accident reports, Deputy Sheriff Albert Rodgers entered and sat down saying, "Afternoon Corporal Younger, Corporal Leeds busy with accidents I see."

Corporal Younger replies, "Afternoon Deputy Rodgers, yes we are and you think people would know slick roads and hitting the breaks is not a good mix."

"Well, some people never learn." The waitress brought the deputy scrambled eggs, bacon, toast and black coffee and they sat around eating.

After ten minutes Deputy Rodgers asks, "Corporal Younger any news on the cult investigation?"

"No Deputy Rodgers. We're looking into some stuff but nothing solid to use and no witnesses."

Deputy Rodgers took off his uniform jacket and Corporal Leeds spotted a tattoo on his right arm and used his foot to nudge Corporal Younger who followed Leeds eyes and saw the tattoo. Younger spoke up, "What are you doing for Christmas eve Deputy Rodgers?"

"Well, I'm working till 9 p.m. then dinner then home why?"

"Me and Sally are having a cop Christmas party and I'm inviting you to it. You can come by after your shift ends."

"Why thank you Peter. I would be honored to attend."

After ten minutes more the deputy finished eating got a coffee to go and left to continue his patrol.

After he left Younger looked at Leeds and said, "Did you get a clear look at the tattoo/ Did it look like the cult one?"

"I'm not sure Peter. It resembled it, but I'm not sure. I would like to be certain before we ruin a career."

They spent thirty more minutes completing the reports, put them in a clip board box, paid for their meals and left to go back on duty. As the afternoon went on they handled two shoplifting calls and lectured the people and took the stuff back and issued a trespass warning then released them. They checked on three elderly residents to make sure they were ok and they had heat and food.

The two officers drove back to the station to file the paperwork and do even more paperwork. As they typed up the reports Younger made a note of Deputy Rodgers badge number and made a note to check it against the list the assistant chief had. It was about 3 p.m. when they drove to the A&W to have a bite to eat with Sergeant Knight, Lieutenant Thompson and Vice Lieutenant McMiller. As Younger and Leeds entered the diner they saw their three fellow cops at the back table and headed towards it.

As they walked past tables the patrons who knew them said afternoon to them and merry Christmas. They sat down and asked them, "Will you two have the usual?"

"Yes, Susan we'll have the usual." She left with their order.

Sergeant Knight said, "Afternoon Peter, Daniel."

"Afternoon Mike, Lieutenant Thompson, Lieutenant McMiller."

Vice Lieutenant McMiller asked, "What time is the Christmas party at your house Peter?"

"Well lieutenant, it will start at 9 p.m. barring any stuff going down. Officers who are on patrol might stop in say hi and exchange gifts, have a cup of eggnog and go back on patrol.

The cops sat around eating and talking about sports, the weather and the cult murders. Vice Lieutenant McMiller asked, "Peter; where are we on the cult murders?"

"Well Assistant Chief Liebermann has a lead on the police insider and it is a deputy sheriff and a partial badge number. This stays between us or a witness gets killed. He also has a list of deputy sheriffs since 1938 with full badge numbers and were going to make a list and put those men under surveillance. We have a possible suspect, but need more proof before we do anything."

Lieutenant Thompson replies, "Good before you kill a cop's career get the facts and make sure it can stand an appeal. What will you do with the other cultists?"

"We'll hand them over gift wrapped to the city attorney with an iron clad conviction case. I don't want those cultists to get off as they deserve jail or the death penalty."

Just then the radio on Younger's hip sputters with the dispatcher saying, "Attention all units 10-59 in progress corner Third Street and Seventy-fifth Street all units respond code 3." With that they all got up ran to their cars as Sergeant Knight tells the dispatcher, "Car 20, 17, 9 and 5 responding code 3."

All of them then sped off and in ten minutes the four cars arrived seeing two other city units and two sheriff units already there. They stopped and got out and run to the group of police struggling with three men and after ten minutes the three men are cuffed on the ground and as they approached Deputy Rodgers sees them and says, "Lieutenant Thompson. A call came in saying three men were seen trying to drag that man" pointing to a homeless man who Younger recognizes as the town drunk Samuel, "into a panel truck and the victim was fighting back and when the call came in I was close by and called for backup."

The men were searched and it was shown by their tattoo's to be cultists who were looking for a sacrifice. Younger walked over, "You ok Samuel?"

The bruised man looks up saying, "Yes, I am Corporal Younger. These young punks messed with a WW2 marine recon man who was in the Pacific campaigns and I am not as young as I once was."

"Well, Deputy Rodgers will take you to the hospital Samuel then to your rooming house. I'll have cars drive by and make sure you're ok." At 5 p.m. Christmas eve Younger hears Samuel is at his rooming house.

It was Christmas eve 1948 and Corporal Younger was driving the patrol car with his partner Corporal Leeds and Sergeant Knight. It was a light snowy night and the dash clock said 6:45 p.m... Another hour Younger thought to himself. They checked the doors of the bank and liquor store and other buildings.

Nearing Sixth Street they saw the town drunk Samuel shivering in a doorway. Younger pulled up and rolled down the window and asked, "Samuel can you come over here?"

The man walked over, "Evening Corporal Younger, cold night isn't it?"

"Why are you out in the cold? Did Miss Parker lock you out again?" Samuel got drunk and forgot to pay his weekly rent.

Younger added, "Get in and we'll go to Miss Parkers rooming house and see what we can do."

Samuel got into the squad car and closed the door and Corporal Younger drove the block and a half to the rooming house and parked out front. All four men got out and approached the door and knocked on the door.

A voice asked, "Who is it?"

"It's Corporal Younger, Leeds and Sergeant Knight and Samuel; can we come in?"

The door opened and a dumpy round woman of fifty stood there and asked, "Come in officers."

They entered and she closed the door and turned on the four men and muttered, "Is Samuel in trouble again?"

Corporal Leeds responded, "No Miss Parker he's not. We spotted him shivering in a doorway and he told us since he didn't pay his weekly rent he was put out."

"Yes, that's correct he owes $20.00 for the week and $20. For the week before."

Officer Younger reached into his wallet and opened it and took out $200 and gave it to her replying, "This should cover him for two months, can I get a receipt?"

Miss Parker looked surprised and Samuel started to cry. Corporal Younger looked at him saying, "Look its Christmas and you're a good man and its too cold outside and this is my Christmas gift."

After getting the receipt the three cops left and when they got back into the squad car Sergeant Knight spoked up," That was nice of you Peter, you surprised me."

"Well Mike, I like to help others when the reason is just, and I didn't want Samuel freezing to death. You of all people can relate to his situation."

Corporal Younger looked at his fellow cops and replied, "Lets go check out and head to my house for the Christmas party."

There were ten city police and seven sheriff department people and their families, The party music was on and everyone was in good spirits. Corporal Younger, Leeds and their women were talking to the sheriff and chief who for the night dropped their feud with each other.

"Chief Carter. What do you plan on doing for the new year?" The sheriff asked.

"Well Davids, hoping I can catch the cult crazies so 1949 will be murder free. I can't stand crazy killers they give me indigestion."

"I can agree with that." Mayor Burk said as he approached the group. "I am up for reelection in 1949 and I need to protect the voters' sorry citizens or I'm getting fired."

Deputy Sheriff Rodgers was drinking a cup of eggnog and Deputy Sheriff Andrews and Sergeant Knight approached and Sergeant Knight asked, "Why are you looking so grim Deputy Rodgers?"

"Well, I received some bad news and I'm not sure how to handle it Sergeant Knight."

"Would you like to talk about it?"

"No thanks. I'm keeping this close to the vest." With that Deputy Rodgers puts the cup down and grabs his uniform jacket and walks up to Corporal Younger and saying, "Thanks for inviting me, but I need to get back on duty." With that he left.

Sergeant Knight said to Corporal Younger, "You think he suspects were onto him?"

"No Mike. He isn't onto us, but we do need to watch him closely."

The night went on the eggnog flowed and the Christmas music played and at 10:30 p.m. everyone exchanged gifts and they partied till 1 a.m. when everyone left. Sally with Leslie went with Younger up to the bedroom to have sex and go to sleep. Sally said to Peter, "That was a good party and everyone had fun."

"Yes, Sally they did. The three of us are drunk what do you want to do next?"

They proceeded to have sex with Younger tied spread eagle to the bed and Leslie and Sally fucking and sucking him.

Two of the cults enforcers bring in a man of twenty-five to Lisa Planetello the cults high priestess saying, "High priestess. We found the member who spray painted the police officers car that brought the heightened search for us."

They shoved him to the floor at her feet and she looked at the scared shaking man with a cold stern look saying in a deadly cold voice, "Why did you do this? Were you trying to get us caught? Now I need to decide your punishment,"

The man crawls to her sobbing, "Please, please high priestess don't kill me. I messed up, but please don't kill me. Turn me over to the police and I'll confess to the deed saying I hate cops and that's why I did it. I won't mention you."

The high priestess thinks to herself how do I punished him? What would fit the crime?"

Just then the phone rings and one of the cult members answers it. "Yes, what is it?"

A voice says on the other end, "The cops know who the man is who spray painted Corporal Youngers car and have a warrant out for him, tell the high priestess." With that the cult member hangs up the phone.

The cult member says, "High priestess, The cops know who spray painted Corporal Youngers car and have a warrant out that was our spy with the sheriff's department."

She turns to the man still on the floor pondering do I turn him in and tell him to confess that he did it on his own, but he does know where we are and who killed the last two sacrifices. She yells, "TIE HIM TO THE ALTER NOW THEN LEAVE."

The two cultists drag him to the blood-stained altar and tie him to it and left. She locks the door, strips off her cloths and puts on the surgical gown and gloves. He knew he was dead. She walks over to the table by the altar picks up a surgical scalpel and cuts the man's cloths off muttering, "vent, omnipoyens aeteme diabelos, lauxnome den; adlo sataana la piet brianta, mo grvtos animon (come almighty eternal devil in the name of our god, Satan the most illuminated, I'll bow to you.)

She takes her sacrificial knife heating it up in a flaming pot till its read hot then slashes his chest twice, as he screams, she climbs on top of his face making him eat her pussy and it stifles the crying as she uses the knife to cut his chest and stomach opening him from both shoulders to the breast bone and as she cums with pleasure and after doing more cutting after she has enough orgasms she climbs off and cuts out his tongue.

She starts to do more cutting and as the blood spurts out as his heart beats on. She then reaches into his stomach and cuts out his liver, then both kidneys and his intestines into the flaming pot saying, "Lord Moloch accept these offerings." Then she uses a bone saw and cuts his rib cage open and pulls out his still beating heart and drinking some blood from it puts it into the flaming pot saying, "Lord Satan accept this heart."

With that she uses the bone saw to cut him up putting his severed body parts in a red biohazard bag. After that's done, she removes the blood spotted surgical gloves and gown dropping them into the flaming pot. She then hoses the blood down the floor drain gets dressed and has the remains dropped into the hospital dumpster and leaves to tell the high priest the problem was solved.

Corporal Younger and his two women fall asleep and at 7 a.m. on December 26, 1948, they get up took a shower and ate breakfast and while Leslie goes to open her shop, Sally leaves to open her beauty parlor. As Corporal Younger enters the locker room, he sees several fellow officers looking rough and jokily says, "What's this the cast of the living dead?"

Officer Michales said, "Morning Peter; have a heart we had a bad night."

"I see that. Just make sure your awake and be ready it's going to be a busy day." With that laughing he leaves the locker room in uniform walking to meet his partner Corporal Leeds for roll call.

Lieutenant Hammond is doing roll call "O.K. officers were going to be busy. Officers Younger and Leeds your car 73 you're going to serve ten warrants for theft, vandalism and checking the business along 75th Street for burglars. Car 62 is Officers Reed and Jacobs you're patrolling the south end of the city be on the look out for Jimmy Ray Thompson age 42, 5"6' we all know who he is, he's wanted by vice for questioning, Car 17B is Sergeant Malcome you're going to be patrol supervisor. Finally, car 5 Officers Williams and Anderson you're patrolling the north end of the city and Officer Thompson your assigned to vice. The rest of you patrol the city and be careful out there. "With that the officers leave for their cars.

It was a cold 39 degrees when Corporals Younger and Leeds walked to their car.and Leeds looked at his breath and said at least our car has heat. Poor Officer Samuels has foot patrol around Parkland Park, we should bring him some coffee."

Younger and Leeds drive to the last known addresses to serve the warrants and by 1 p.m. had served all warrants taking all seventeen men and six women into custody. At 2 p.m. they see Officer Samuels walking on patrol and Leeds driving pulls along side and says, "Afternoon Alexander; we have some coffee for you get in."

Officer Samuels replied, "Thanks Dan, I do appreciate it, its cold out." Younger hands Samuels a large cup of coffee and a thermos and sitting in the car the three-officer talk about nothing.

After thirty minutes Samuels says, "Thanks Peter, Dan I need to get back om patrol."

Younger and Leeds don't see the suspicious figure watching them from a doorway and the figure tries to stay out of sight. They ran into Sheriff Davids and Deputy McAllister and pulled alongside their car and Younger rolls down the window saying, "Afternoon Sheriff Davids, Deputy McAllister."

The sheriff replied, "Afternoon Corporal Younger, Leeds cold day, isn't it?"

Corporal Younger replies, "Yes, it is sheriff. We're just glad not to be on foot patrol."

"Any updates on the cult murder investigation?" Deputy McAllister asked.

"No deputy, nothing new. Were still trying to identify the layers and we'll let the sheriff and Chief Carter know when we have something."

"Please keep me in the loop Younger. I want to find out who the traitor is in my department." the sheriff said.

"Will do sheriff, you'll be the first to know, right after we tell the chief." With that they pull off to continue their patrol. There passing Shermans Christian Book Store. The owner was on vacation and asked the cops to keep an eye on this business. They pulled past the shop and called for back up. Two more cars in ten minutes pulled up and they took positions.

Younger and Leeds covered the back door and Davis and Parker covered the front and Lewis and Miller backed them up, On the count of three the cops entered the shop and caught three masked men vandalizing the place and after some resistance by the burglars all three were in cuffs.

Younger and Leeds stood the men up and pulled off the masks and said, "You are under arrest."

Officer Leeds notices a tattoo on the arm of one of the men and got his partners attention. Younger who was searching the other two finds they also have that tattoo. The three burglars are silent as the officers waited for the paddy wagon. While Officers Davis and Parker stay at the store waiting for the owner the other officers head back to the station to do reports. The figure following Corporal Younger was mad and left to have a talk with the high priest.

The figure appeared in front of the high priest and angerly said, "Three of your followers stupidly burglarized a religious bookstore and got caught, your church is about to be discovered."

The high priest told hid god, "How dare you..." Before he could finish a power blast launched him five feet into a wall telling him, "I am the Lord Molech, and you will never talk to me in that tone you insolent servant or I'll kill you and find someone who will obey orders understand!"

The priest replies from the floor, "Yes lord Molech I understand and apologize."

The high priestess and two cult members stood scared at their god's presence and menacing. The god turns to the other cult members and yells, "GET THIS PIECE OF DUNG OUT OF MY SIGHT." pointing to the high priest cowering and adds, "any more failures and you will feel my wrath."

Thy all-leave trembling and the god is thinking to himself these followers are dung. I need to get rid of them. That police officer wants them caught. I need to visit him. These dung beetles are not important I can get others that will follow my commands."

# Chapter Six

To say Lord Molech was pissed off at the high priest and priestess who disrespected him by making them higher than him. Lord Molech thought to himself, *I'm a realist, I reward those who serve me and follow my commands and I only want three sacrifices year. Any more in this current age brings problems. I'm tired of them and I know what to do.*

Lord Molech decided to turn those dung Beatles over to Corporal Younger and rid himself of this baggage. Later that night he visits Corporal Younger who is sleeping and wakes him up by saying, "Wake up Corporal Younger I want to speak with you."

Corporal Younger opens his eyes and stares in horror at the god Molech standing at the foot of the bed looking at him with dark flaming eyes.

"Relax you are safe. I have a gift for you. The former high priest and priestess and their members you are hunting have disobeyed me and my commands and I am done with them. There are more deserving followers. I'll tell you where their latest sacrifice will be done."

"Why tell me this? Why help me?"

"You are honorable and seek to do justice and I only ordered them to do three sacrifices a year and only the unwanted people who won't be missed. They have vexed me, and I am done with them. Go to 743 Parkland Drive West on the evening of 17 January 1949 and justice will be served and questions answered."

"What do you want in return for this help?"

"Nothing just get rid of these ungrateful, disobedient dung and cleanse the world of these worthless worms."

"I will do just that and thank you for the information. You're the first God I've met and not what I expected."

"I am a rational god. I have my wants and desires and demand obedience and hate followers who see them higher than me. I'll go now and let you go back to sleep."

Before Younger knows it's 8 a.m. and the dream he decides was it real or imagined? But the god Molech gave him the information I wanted, but should I tell the other? Since there were four weeks till this event, he decides to keep it to himself. After waking up Younger said to Sally when she asked, "Why are you shivering," Sally asks, "What's wrong Peter?"

"You wouldn't believe me if I told you."

"Try me, Peter."

"Well, the god Molech who those cultists worship visited ma and gave me the time and place of their next sacrifice. They pissed their god off by elevating themselves above him. I am not sure how to tell my partner about this."

"Just level with him. You've been partnering for a long time, don't keep silent."

The morning of December 27 1948, started off a cold twenty-four degrees and Corporal Younger was still confused about the gods visit early this morning and opened Corporal Leeds believed him.

After roll call as they left the police garage in their patrol car driving down Sixty-Third street towards Eighteenth Street Corporal Younger turns to his partner and said, :Dan you may or may not believe me, but the god those cultists worship came to me earlier this morning and offered to give the cult group and its leaders up to me; he even gave me the date, time and location of their next sacrifice."

His partner turns and replies, "Did he tell you the name of the deputy sheriff in with the cult?"

"No, he did not. He figures if we remove the cult for good that person would be alone and no threat to anyone."

"Do we wait till a week from the date to tell the others?"

"Yes, Dan we wait. I want to be sure we do it right. I want to cruise by the address in an unmarked car and check it out first and then decide how many cops we'll need. There are fifteen members of the cult including the high priest and priestess."

As they drive on the dispatcher calls out, "Car 24, car 24 handle a 10-32 just occurred corner of Seventh Street and Sixty-Fifth Street handle code two. Units 7B and 15 are also enroute."

Corporal Leeds picks up the mike saying, "Rodger dispatch enroute." As Younger hits the lights and speeds to the location.

In ten minutes, they arrive and see units 7B and 15 ae there with the hospital ambulance crew. They pull up and see a man about thirty-five down on the cols ground with the ambulance crew and the doctor attending to him. As they approach, they see Lieutenant Powell taking the man's statement. The ambulance crew puts the man on a stretcher and load him up and speed off to the hospital three blocks west.

Lieutenant Powell informs Younger and Leeds of the events. "Randolph Miller aged 35 was walking home and was jumped by two men he gave me their descriptions and I know these two punks. Joe Alexander age 31 5'6" black with scar on left cheek and R.J. singleton aged 31."

Younger asks, "Were there any witnesses? Did anyone see it?"

"Yes, Ms. Baxter looked out of her window and saw it happen. I have her statement. I am going back to headquarters to get warrants." Lieutenant Powell replies.

Corporal Leeds asks, "Why warrants lieutenant? We know who and have a witness lets just go get them."

"Well, the first punk Alexander is the son of the vice mayor, so I want to keep it all legal."

The lieutenant heads back to the station and Younger and Leeds go back on patrol. The rest of the day was uneventful with little to no calls.

At 3:30 p.m. on December 27th they stop for lunch at the Burger Barn.

As they entered several of the patrons greeted the two officers and the waitress names Margret asks, "Afternoon Corporal Younger, Leeds the usual?"

Corporal Leeds replies, "Yes Margret the usual." Both cops sat at a table in the back and were drinking coke while their food was cooked.

Five minutes later the waitress brought Younger his double cheese-burger, fries and Leeds triple burger with cheese and fries. As they eat Leeds says to his partner, "Peter what are you doing New Year's Eve?"

"Well Dan I got duty to make sure the drunks don't kill anybody by doing a roadblock on the main road in Tillman."

As the city hall clock struck 3 p.m. Younger and Leeds were driving down Central Boulevard towards Seventy-fifth street and at the corner of Seventy-fifth and Central they saw a strange black figure 7" tall no features pointing at them. Leeds stopped the car and turned to Peter saying, "What the hell is that?"

"I don't know Dan, but it makes my blood run cold." After three minutes it vanishes.

The morning on January 1, 1949, Younger processed the last of the forty people arrested for DWI. He wanted to go check on Leslie as she was acting strange, avoiding him and Sally and being a lot darker than she used to be. He couldn't understand she vanished for days on end and when she returned, she was stranger and stranger. He wanted to follow her but was scared she'd take it as he didn't trust her.

He decided to stop by her apartment and check on her, he decided to keep Sally out of this.

As he pulled up to Leslie's apartment, he felt a darker feeling coming from the door. He knocked on the door and then a voice said, "Who is it?"

"Leslie its Peter. I wanted to check on you."

The door opened and Leslie was in her usual lace lingerie outfit with lace gloves, but instead of blue, pink, red or white it was jet black and she wore black lipstick. He shivered.

Leslie said, "I'm glad you came Peter I missed our sex, and I missed dominating you, please come in."

Peter entered and Leslie shut and locked the door, and he noticed the feeling in the apartment was dark and evil. She walked up behind him and wrapped her arms around him and kissed him full and deep on the lips. She asked, "How was that?"

Peter replied, "That last kiss could level a small country."

She smiled and replied, "Its sex time Peter." She took him by the hand into the bedroom and it was candlelit with blackout drapes over the windows and the usual under the bed restraints. She said, "Strip Peter I need your dick and cum."

As he stripped, he shivered and as she tied him spread eagle and took off the lace gloves and put on a pair of black sterile surgical gloves and she sat on the bed and while deep kissing him her hands ran over his body, and he got extremely aroused. Leslie looked at his swollen engorged penis licking her lips and ran tongue up and down while stroking it.

Peter was whimpering and moaning as she did it faster and deeper more than she had done before, She stopped and sat her pussy over his mouth and while he ate her pussy she sucked and stroked till all the cum came out of his balls and after one hour she climbed off and smiled at him and she climbed on his dick and fucked him till he was begging her to stop. She laughed and refused and after seven hours he laid there unable to move, She untied him and said, "You were better than usual."

"You changed Leslie you got darker more aggressive, colder and giving evil vibes, what's up?"

"My new friends do things to me, and I find it impossible to get them to stop."

"Let me know who they are, and I'll get them to stop."

"I know you would Peter, but for some reason I can't allow that."

They took a shower together and ate breakfast and Leslie said, "Thank you for coming over. I needed your sexual energy badly. Thank you for your concerns." With that he left and decided he was going to put her under surveillance to see what's up."

Corporal Younger went to Chief Carter and told him about the dark gods visit and giving up the location where the next human sacrifice was to be, The chief asked, "What do you need?"

"I need to put Leslie Pattached under surveillance as I believe the cult will either use her as a sacrifice or have recruited her, I am not sure which."

Chief Carter picks the phone up, "Lieutenant Patrick could you come to my office?"

Ten minutes later Chief Carter briefs him on everything and Corporal Younger chimed in saying, "I need her to be watched as she is either a witness in the cult murders or joined the cult. I know the budget is tight, but I know the date, time and place of the next cult kill."

Corporal younger on leaving tells the lieutenant and chief, "Don't tell the sheriff."

# Chapter Seven

Corporal Younger leaves the chief's office and runs into Sergeant Knight and says, "Afternoon Mike."

"Afternoon Peter. I hear the cult case has gotten weird."

Sergeant Knight sees the surprise on Corporal Younger's face and says, "Relax the sheriff don't know. Dan filled me in. The secret is safe."

"Yes, Mike it has gotten weird. I just hope that God was correct as those worshipers apparently are not obeying his commands and might do something crazy."

Both men walk to the patrol division to see if Corporal Leeds was there. They enter the office and see Leeds on the phone as they approach, he says, "Peter there was another murder and the patrol unit on scene says it was a cult killing."

"How do they know the cult's responsible?"

"They caught the murderer, and they were forced to kill him after he charged them with a machete. Both men had cult tattoos on them."

"Was it a sacrifice?"

"No, it was a straight up killing, and the victim was another cultist."

It was p p.m. on the 2$^{nd}$ of January and as Corporal Younger entered his home Sally greeted him. She asks him, "How was work?"

He replied, "The usual nothing serious just patrolling and serving warrants."

"Why hasn't Leslie been over? Has she tired of us?"

"She has stuff going on and decided to deal with it alone. I offered to help, and she said no." He did not tell Sally of Leslie's darker ways and concerns that he couldn't trust her.

He ate a late dinner with Sally then they watched TV, a new invention till 11:30 p.m. then both went upstairs to bed. Peter and Sally had sex there was no bondage, but Sally did wear latex medical gloves and force Peter to eat her pussy as she gave him a deep gloved blow job. Sal-

ly told Peter, "Get on top of me and fuck me how much you like me."
So, he slid his hard thick dick into her hot, wet blond pussy and started off slow and soon he had Sally moaning and crying out and the bed
creaked as she wanted more.

After four hours Sally rolled Peter on his back and missionary
fucked him. She spoke Latin and Peter asked her, "I didn't know you
spoke Latin."

She replied, "I don't. You should know that, why do you ask?"

"No reason." This was another strange event he needed to figure
out. As he slept, he had a dream where the God Molech visited him and
told him where the high priest could be found.

After he got up at 6 a.m. he realized the god really wanted them
gone. So, he wrote down the address 73 A Street. He got up, showered,
got dressed and told Sally he had to leave for work as something came
up.

It was January 4, 1949 when he entered the station and went to
the detective division and saw Sergeant Knight and Lieutenant Powell.
"Morning Mike, Lieutenant I got some information we need to act fast
upon. I just found out where the cults high priest is hiding out."

"How did you get this information?" Lieutenant Powell asked.

Looking at Sergeant Knight Corporal Younger said simply, "Did
you tell him?"

"No Peter I did not; you wanted to keep it quiet."

"Well lieutenant the god those cultists worship is pissed at them
and wants them gone as they are disobeying him, and he gave me the
location of the high priest earlier this morning and when their next sacrifice is going to happen."

Lieutenant Powell replies, "Well let's get two other units and hit
the place before he flees."

So, Lieutenant Powell, Sergeant Knight, Corporal Younger and
Leeds and four of Lieutenant Powell's squad and headed to 73 A Street.
It was 8 a.m. when they had the address surrounded and decided to

hit the front door and rear door at the same time while the two other units watched the windows. At 8:15 on January fourth the front and back door was kicked in and the cops yelled, "TILLMAN POLICE EVERYONE RAISE YOUR HANDS."

In ten minutes, they had the high priest and two cultists and tons of evidence on three murders the police were investigating. Two of the newspaper reporters showed up and took pictures of the people arrested and got some statements from the cops. Lieutenant Powell asked the reporters, "Can you hold off till the evening edition?"

Both reporters replied, "Since were the only ones here yes we can do that."

The cults high priest and two cultists were put in the paddy wagon and taken to police headquarters and charged with seven counts first degree murder with special circumstances, six counts kidnapping and upon being booked and mug shots taken they were immediately taken before the arraignment judge. As they led the three cultists into the court from in waist and ankle shackles the court bailiff says, "Case 49-1763 the State of Nebraska, City of Tillman vs. Edward Malcolm, Samuel O'Neill and Paul Donaldson arrested on seven counts murder in the first with special circumstances, six counts kidnapping."

The judge asks the three men, "How do you pled?"

All three say not guilty. The judge asks the city attorney, "Views on bail?"

"Remand your honor. These men murdered seven people in cold blood by human sacrifice and dismembering. They are a threat to society."

The judge then says, "All three are remanded to the city jail till their trial date of 11 January 1949 8 a.m. in this court room; next case."

The high priest turns to Corporal Younger and asks, "How did you find us?"

Corporal Younger replied, "Your god. You pissed him off so badly he wanted to destroy your whole cult and you but gave you to me and the cops. You should never piss off a god."

As Corporal Younger left the courthouse the city attorney asks him, "What is the high priestess and the rest of the cult going to do?"

"Well, we know the date of their next sacrifice and their god hasn't told me of any other stuff. We have that address on surveillance. We just have to wait."

The sheriff walks up to Corporal Younger, "Why didn't you let me know?"

"Well sheriff I had to act fast to catch them before they fled. I am working on more information, and I almost have the address of their next sacrifice. I'll let you know the time and place."

"How about I assign Deputy Sheriff Albert Rodgers to help you?"

"Thanks, but I don't trust him. He has a cult tattoo on his right wrist and he nay or may not be active, but I don't want to chance it."

"He does? I never saw it."

"He kept it covered by his uniform shirt. I will keep you informed sheriff. I am trying to keep the investigation close to the vest, so he protected from interference."

"Ok but keep me informed as I don't want crooked cops in my department."

Corporal Younger sat in the locker room, and he felt a presence and the God Molech appeared and said, "They moved the date up to January 6th as they still hope to get me to help them. I am not going to do it." He then vanished; it was January 4, 1949.

Corporal Younger thought oh shit, I need to jump on this. He ran to the homicide division and saw Lieutenant Powell, Corporal Leeds, and Sergeant Knight. He rushed in exclaiming, "The God Molech came to me the cult is moving the date to January 6th we need to act fast. We have two days."

Lieutenant Powell says, "Corporal Younger go and infiltrate the cult if you can since they don't exactly know what you like."

Corporal Younger thought I hope they don't know me ot I'll be in trouble. He went in a unmarked car to see the surveillance team.

He pulled up behind the two cops in a unmarked car and walked up and opened the back door saying, "Afternoon Jim, Randy. Anything going on?"

Officer Jim Ingles and randy Reed turned and replied, "Afternoon Peter, No nothing yet."

Officer Ingles added, "Well, there was a dark figure very evil looking entering the house walking through the wall. It got our attention."

"I've seen the same entity it made my blood run cold." Younger replied.

They sat there for ten minutes when the high priestess and four men in robes entered the house.

"The sacrifice is set for January 6$^{th}$ looks like their getting ready." Younger replied.

He got out of the car and walked to his car and drove off. He decided to stop by Leslie's shop and check on her. As he pulls up to her shop and gets out of the car and upon entering sees Leslie looking troubled. "HI Leslie. Anything I can help you with?"

"Hi Peter. No there is nothing. I am glad you're checking on me." She replied walking up to him and they kissed.

"Why can't you trust me enough to tell me what's wrong."

"I just can't Peter. I don't want you to get hurt."

"What makes you think it will hurt me?"

"I don't know. I just know I don't want you involved, good by Peter." With that he leaves her shop slightly hurt that after all they had done, she still won't trust him.

He heads back to the police station wondering what is going on with Leslie. He stopped by the local Shell station to fill his unmarked patrol car when a sheriff; s car with Deputy Sheriff Albert Rodgers driving who pulls up rolls down his window saying, "Afternoon Corporal Younger/"

'Afternoon Deputy Rodgers. Cold day, isn't it?"

"Yes, it is. It's supposed to get up to 45 degrees tomorrow."

"That will be good I have always hated cold weather."

"Well, I got to get back on patrol talk to you later."

After filling up he returns to the police station to do reports. He pulls into the parking lot and parks and gets out. A male figure walks up to him and says, "Corporal Younger don't turn around we need to talk. I know who the dirty cop is in the sheriff's department and I'm going to tell you, but I want something in return."

"What do you want?'

"I want immunity. I never took part in the cult's human sacrifices and me and the high priestess had a fight. I stand with our god, and she don't. I found out she wants to kill me."

"Are you the upcoming human sacrifice?"

"No. I don't know who it is. Do we have a deal?"

"Let me have the name and I'll quietly investigate and if true I'll see to it you get immunity."

"Ok. I'll trust you. The name is Deputy Sheriff Allen Rodgers. He has a cult tattoo on his left back wrist, Be careful he's dangerous."

"Did he join in the human sacrifices?"

"No. Like me he's loyal to our god. So, no he did not."

"OK, some stuff you tell me matches information I have, so let me get with the sheriff and city attorney. How do I reach you?"

"If immunity is approved hang a red cloth in your front window for yes."

With that the unknown man walked off. Corporal Younger already suspected Deputy Rodgers now fact is known. He had to get to the sheriff and city attorney.

He goes into the police station and calls the city attorney and sheriff to meet him in Chief Carters office as he has major information on the cult murders and to keep this secret.

Twenty minutes later the city attorney, Sheriff Davids, Chief Carter, Sergeant Knight, Corporal Younger and Leeds, Lieutenant Powell were in the office,

"Well, everyone I got the name of the crooked deputy sheriff from a member of the cult and he was told by their god to turn the deputy in. District attorney he wants immunity from prosecution to testify in open court on the deputy and he's not connected with the cult murders."

"If this checks out, I have no problem with immunity, but only if I can get a conviction."

"I'll let him know. Sheriff Davids the deputy in question is Deputy Allen Rodgers. He has a cult tattoo, and the witness will testify that he'd seen Deputy Rodgers participation in two unknown murders."

"Why that evil bastard. I'll deal with him very fast."

"Wait sheriff. We want him alive and to testify against the high priest for a open and shut case." The city attorney chimes in.

"OK, I'll go get him."

Corporal Younger adds, "Let's let our internal affairs and yours to go get him so it doesn't look like its biased." With that they all leave. Corporal Younger, Leeds and two men from the city police and two from the sheriff department internal affairs department leave in cars to go get Deputy Rodgers.

At 4:30 p.m. on January 4th the team pulls up to where Deputy Rodgers is eating lunch in his car and Lieutenant Hiller from the sheriff's department internal affairs says as the deputy rolls down the window, "Your under arrest Rodgers for three counts murder in the first. Please get out of the car."

All of a sudden Deputy Rodgers pulls his service revolver and tries to shoot Lieutenant Hiller and Corporal Leeds, but Corporal Younger shoots Deputy Rodgers twice. Younger knew the sheriff and city attorney wouldn't be happy.

After the crime scene people photographed everything and a team from the Nebraska State Patrol took charge and wrote up the reports, took statements and turned it over to the city and county district attorneys.

When the high priest heard that a member of his cult had killed himself instead of being arrested and questioned, he was happy. A voice out of nowhere said, "Don't get happy. You're done for."

The high priest asked, "Who are you?"

The voice said, "Your God."

The high priest then realized he was in very serious trouble. He needed his high priestess to help him out of jail.

The morning of January 5, 1949, started off a cold 17 degrees as Corporal Younger drove into the station. As he got out of the car a voice said, "You forgot to put the red cloth in your window. What did the city attorney say?"

"If he can get straight testimony that convicts the high priest then it is yes. I also want to see your face."

"Turn around Younger." Corporal Younger turns around and sees the face of Commissioner of Public Works Alex Green.

Upon seeing the surprise on Corporal Youngers face he said, "It was about power and greed, but no murders."

"Didn't you know what you were getting into?"

"I knew in times past they did human sacrifices, but while I was there, I never seen them doing one. I don't like how they threw our god to the curb and set themselves as gods."

"Will you let me know the date and place of the cults next sacrifices?"

"I'll try, but the high priest and priestess and two others only know that information." With that the man leaves Younger thinks to himself

I'm glad I know the time, place and date. With that he enters the police station to start his shift.

While on patrol with his partner Corporal Leeds and Sergeant Knight who was tagging along but didn't give a reason.

Corporal Leeds turns his head and asks Sergeant Knight, "Mike. What's with the ride along?"

"Can I just ride along with fellow cops? Do I need to have a reason?"

"Yes Mike. You always have a reason."

"Well, ok. You pissed someone off Peter. The chief picked up a rumor that someone wants you dead or at least in the hospital. The chief asked me to ride with you two just to be safe."

"It's the cult. One of their members was the one who gave me the information that he'd like to testify against their high priest. If any of the cult found out wouldn't they just kill him? Why me?"

"Well, you're more of a threat. Don't worry I believe their god will keep you safe. Wait, why did I say that?"

It was the morning of January 6, 1949, the day of the human sacrifice. He decided to go undercover by sneaking into the house. He didn't tell the chief or others about this.

He knew he shouldn't do this, by the had to peak in. As he sneaked around the outside of the house a voice in his head said *Watch out look behind you!* He turned in time to see the high priestess about to stab him. They collided and were wrestling around on the ground and Corporal Younger broke her neck. He stood up and found an open door and went in.

Corporal Younger still never believed in witchcraft or satanic power, but as he watched the four men in a room only lit with bright candles and Leslie Pattached tied to an altar gagged and whimpering in terror as the men surrounded her and when the with the blue robes spoke he said, "Oh dark god accept this sacrifice and her blood to help save your son who is to be sentenced to death; use the blood and death energy of this sacrifice to help free him."

The man dropped the hood of his robe and Younge saw the face of the Undersheriff Johnny Belvidere. The others also dropped their hoods and he saw the faces of Alex Green the City Commissioner of Public Works and Phillip Matthews City School Board Superintendent and a man Younger didn't recognize.

He realized he needed to act and as the four raised their knives he burst through the door and yelled, "TILLMAN POLICE DROP THE WEAPONS OR YOUR DEAD! YOUR UNDER ARREST>"

He saw in a split second before the knives descended to kill Leslie and with six shots, he killed the men. He went up to Leslie and said, "Don't move I'll untie you."

After he untied Leslie's hands and legs, he noticed her jump up grabbing a knife about to stab him when a voice yelled, "WATCH OUT YOUNGER!" with that two shots rang out and Leslie died. He turned to see Sheriff Jack Davids entering with two deputies.

"Sorry we almost didn't get here sooner Corporal Younger. Traffic kept us. You're wondering how I knew about this?"

Younger asked, "Yes sheriff I do."

"Well, I suspected my undersheriff of doing satanic worship but couldn't prove it till five hours ago. I interrogated the high priest about this."

"What now sheriff?" Younger asked.

"Well, we'll write this up as a case of kidnapping, serial sexual assault and brain washing for the women; for the men we'll just leave it as four mentally unhinged men tried to kill a woman in a misguided belief in the power to save a criminal with her death."

The papers the next day praised the sheriff and Corporal Younger and the cult leader was sentenced to death. He was executed on January 25, 1949, and soon forgotten about.

Thank you for buying and reading this fifth book in the A Kiss Before Strangling series. Please leave a review.

Milton Keynes UK
Ingram Content Group UK Ltd.
UKHW020014040624
443552UK00013B/409